The Word Book

Originally published in Japanese as *Tangoshu* by Chikuma Shobo, Tokyo, 1979
Copyright © Mieko Kanai, 1979
Translation copyright © Paul McCarthy, 2009
First English translation, 2009

Library of Congress Cataloging-in-Publication Data

Kanai, Mieko, 1947-
[Tangoshu. English]
The word book / Mieko Kanai ; translated by Paul McCarthy.
    p. cm.
"Originally published in Japanese as Tangoshu by Chikuma Shobo, Tokyo, 1979"--T.p.
verso.
ISBN 978-1-56478-566-4 (pbk. : alk. paper)
I. McCarthy, Paul. II. Title.
PL855.A52T3613 2009
895.6'35--dc22
                    2009018378

Partially funded by a grant from the Illinois Arts Council, a state agency, and by the University of Illinois at Urbana-Champaign

This book has been selected by the Japanese Publishing Project (JLPP), an initiative of the Agency for Cultural Affairs of Japan.

www.dalkeyarchive.com

Cover: design and composition by Danielle Dutton, art by Nicholas Motte
Printed on permanent/durable acid-free paper and bound in the United States of America

The Word Book   Mieko Kanai
translated by Paul McCarthy

Dalkey Archive Press
Champaign & London

Rivals

I was having my second meal of the day in the empty dining car (there was only one other customer) on the express train heading north. I had eaten a good breakfast at the inn that morning but had failed to eat lunch, what with the troublesome transfers from plane to train. Besides, I have found at times that I have an almost shamefully large appetite, and such was the case on that particular day. I consumed two portions of a light gratin of the scallops famous in the area, then the roast beef that was another regional specialty, a green asparagus salad, and peach sherbet. On the table was a water glass containing a pink carnation and some asparagus leaves. Why are carnations always paired with asparagus leaves, I wondered for a moment, but then the all-too-obvious answer came to me: carnations have artificial-looking, perfectly straight stems with just a few meager leaves attached, mustache-like, so unless you have a great many of them, they look very skimpy. The thin lacey green of the asparagus leaves forms a still more artful "dress" for the artificial-looking carnations. That was the boring, commonplace conclusion I came to.

As I finished the meal and started on my coffee, the sun began to set beyond the forest. The whole area was enveloped in pale rose-colored shadows and emitted a faint silvery light. The scenery outside the train window moved by at a regular pace; there were no electric lights to give a hint of human habitation. Only the broad plain (said to be wasteland); and the evergreen forest, which seemed even now to be struggling to expand its domain, if only by a little, against that wasteland; and the brook running forlornly along the bottom of a craggy valley that appeared to have been abruptly carved out of the forested zone by some sudden fracture of the earth; and the small gnarled shrubs that grew everywhere, clinging to the cracks in the rocks and putting forth yellow flowers. My eyes took pleasure in the silver radiance glistening like a ribbon of film from the river that threaded its way across the plain in the midst of this rather monotonous scenery, and in the acacia and the pussy willows with their blossoms covered in gray fur precisely like a cat's, and in the varicolored wild flowers—all of which lent a gentleness to the riverbank. All afternoon the train passed through pastureland set with miniature views of cattle in the distance. But once night had fallen, all these delightful scenes only increased the forest's loneliness. As I finished drinking my second cup of coffee, the last faint radiance of dusk was swallowed up by the hills.

As we rounded a curve, the water in the glass with the carnation shifted with the movement of the train, and the carnation shook its head in a sprightly dance. The fatigue from my trip and the pleasant sense of fullness after eating so well made me yawn, and I lit a cigarette. Thinking of a certain person, I smiled for a moment. Had he been here, he might have said, "We seem to be heading for 'the Domain of Arnheim.'" It was his habit to read only the first few pages of a novel, never continuing on. And I would never write anything beyond the opening of a novel—perhaps trying to postpone the "sorrow" of ending something?

It was just then that the man drinking whiskey at the table diagonally across from mine smiled at me. If you find yourself with only one other person in a railway dining car and that person smiles at you, you would have to be a very strong-willed sort of person to ignore it. Now I am by no means strong-willed, so I couldn't help but return his smile vaguely, just enough to be polite.

"Unless you're changing trains at one of the stations along the way, it'll be four hours or more till we reach the end of the line. Won't you have a whiskey with me?" he said. Then he added, "Of course, that's what one is supposed to say if one is glad to find someone to talk to when bored, thus masking one's intrusiveness with a show of good nature."

Why am I so open when it comes to listening to a stranger's story, I wondered. And about how old was this smaller-than-average man wearing a nondescript blue-gray tweed coat that was neither quiet nor loud?

"It's said that people who do this kind of work generally develop the ability to tell a person's character to some extent, simply from external impressions. A kind of intuition that comes from our occupational training, you might say. And, to be sure, a certain mild contempt for people in general, arising from our belief in our own powers of discernment regarding others, is one of the things that helps maintain our self-respect as professionals—though to me it all seems like a lot of hooey. My main reason for liking this kind of work is that it allows me to travel, and another is that what we are going around selling is a kind of catalog of the world. We have to capture the hearts of others with words, the highly romantic power contained in words. We have to take advantage of the romantic fantasies most people have with regard to knowledge. We have to secularize knowledge, make it anonymous, and convince people that the world can be contained in an encyclopedia. In short, we are selling the sweet dream that there is a sure and unchanging 'world of facts' out there centered on the words collected in an encyclopedia. In most families an encyclopedia is regarded as a compilation of unchanging facts. Facts never grow old, so it's a really good buy. But, as you are aware, there's no book that grows old as quickly as an encyclopedia. To give the simplest example: an encyclopedia from ten years ago accurately recorded the population of a given city at the time, but now, ten years later, that city has doubled in size. And that's the way it is with the progress of science, too. Science is a field in which the newest facts are the best, most accurate ones; although with most things, it's just the opposite: the older a thing is, the better, and the more we prize it."

At first we talked about his line of work. "Is this a business trip?" I asked in the usual hackneyed way, and he began to explain his occupation. "Well, then, you must have a lot of luggage," I said, because I sensed that he might be traveling with an entire sample encyclopedia. Of course I did all the listening, since I had no romantic tales to tell about myself—or, if I had, I might have recalled my absurdly sentimental past in response to this external stimulus. I found his conversation very interesting, in a certain way. I've met lots of different types of people in my time. It's not that the numbers have been so great; it's just that in life you have to encounter various types of people, like it or not. And it was not unusual for me to become the listener to their stories—indeed, I rather liked listening to them. All sorts of unusual things, some of them quite abnormal, kept happening, but never to me, only to these others. That made my lonely existence seem still more lonely, but I suppose I must count it as a plus. Because I—no, I really don't have to talk about myself. I am merely the intermediary of this story.

Is it still there, I wonder—that tea room with its little Spanish-style garden in the hotel near the Sengaku-ji temple? You could have your tea in a wisteria-covered pergola, on a terrace floored with alternating matte tiles of pale brown and gray in a chessboard pattern. The hotel itself was a gloomy structure built in a truncated L-shape. Surrounding the small tiled Spanish garden, the one-story wooden tea room, whose thick, dark-brown pillars and white stucco gave it a rustic European look, was attached to the hook of the L like a small brown wen.

One Sunday afternoon in May, starting my stroll from Gyoranzaka, I discovered this quiet café terrace. This discovery intoxicated me as much as the cold Pilsen beer that I drank at the small round stone table in the Spanish garden. I was very young, and May can make you feel terribly nostalgic when you're young. We have nothing to recall, no object for our nostalgia, but still, for that very reason, we feel ourselves overcome with nostalgia as we drowse and doze the hours away.

I remember clearly even now that that was the first time I had entered a shop by myself and ordered something alcoholic to drink.

How had I been able to summon up the courage to do such a thing on that particular day? If I tell you that I had been visiting a beautiful woman who lived near Gyoranzaka, and was quite excited, you will surely understand. It was, in a word, my first love. And only two weeks later (though I doubt anyone remembers the event anymore), a story I had written was praised by a kind and experienced writer-critic, and I made my debut in "the literary world." Just as someone who thinks he might write a story, or in fact is in the process of writing one, may not be a novelist in the true sense, so the fact that someone has written a story does not necessarily mean that he or she is aiming at being a novelist. In my own case, though, it would seem that I really wanted to become a novelist. My next story, and the one after that as well, were well received—it often happens, you know, with young writers, that mature critics will ignore the weaker aspects and make a point of praising the general beauty of the work. And that's how a whole volume of my stories came to be published. This sort of favorable criticism is a kind of duty on the part of the established writers toward the new, younger ones. Besides, it's clear as day to them that if new blood isn't pumped into their world, the continued existence of that world will be endangered. So there's no need to go all weak at the knees because of their kindness. Basically, we've given their old fiction an injection of fresh blood, bursting with energy. What they wanted from us was a youthful sparkle in the eye with just a touch of aggression, the alertness of a hunting dog that is not about to wag its tail at the world as presented. But there seemed to be an unbridgeable gap between their expectations and our spirit. We wanted to defend our own little worlds rather than go on the attack; and vis-à-vis the world as presented, we didn't so much wag our tails as put them firmly between our legs.

However, the real reason we stopped writing fiction was that we had experienced things that made it fundamentally impossible to believe in the "originality" that is demanded of a literary work.

As I mentioned before, I experienced first love, and the woman was completely unconnected with literature. She didn't bother to read the fiction that I, who was so close to her, had written, even from a purely extra-literary curiosity, as I think most women would have done. When I think back, I can come up with a totally different explanation for why I was so wild about her than I could have back then. I think it was because she was the mirror that showed me my rival. Back then (and it really was a long time ago) I believed I was crazy about her body, or rather, the sensuous nature of her very existence. For she, this woman with arms as white as lotus flowers, had led me into a world of sensation such that it was no wonder a young, inexperienced guy like me would go crazy for her.

I realized some other man was paying frequent visits to her house when I discovered a notebook he had left behind in her room. Oddly enough, I felt little jealousy at the time. I'm not so naïve as to expect that I would be the only lover of a beautiful woman. I sensed, rather, in this unknown man's carelessness in leaving behind his handwritten notebook the hope that it would be read by someone. I rebuked that unknown man in exceptionally mocking terms: "If you're that eager to be read, I'll read your damn notebook!"

"But that's someone else's journal!" said the woman. "I think it's a dirty trick to read it on the sly like this." These words, intended to show how "correct" she was, but which made her seem unclean to me, made me even angrier. "He deliberately left his notebook behind because the dirty bastard wanted it read! I'll bet he writes fiction too," I answered. Actually, I suspect I was right about that.

I spirited the notebook out with me and started reading it in the tea room with the Spanish-style terrace, ordering a beer for myself there for the second time.

The notebook contained passages I myself had written, but that does not mean that the unknown man deliberately copied each word and phrase from my book. His notebook was exactly identical to my own. And from then on, whenever I went to her house I would find a notebook containing passages identical to what I had written in my own.

I no longer took the pleasure I once had in the act of writing (or even reading). It was almost incredible to me that there had ever been a time when I had enjoyed doing such things. What I wrote had always already (or simultaneously) been written by someone else—that was the fact of the matter. I would extend my various perceptive feelers toward the world: that is to say, I would write; and feelers similar in shape would appear before me. A person unknown to me would extend those feelers and write. And I would read what he had written. If I wrote "I wrote," the unknown writer of the notebook would record there "I wrote." This happened with every passage and every word I wrote, and I was pained by the unbelievable thought that it would continue to happen. The peculiar experience of reading my own words as something someone else had written caused me much pain. I seemed to be involved in endless rivalry with him. I stopped using the word "I." I'm sure you understand: you can imagine how meaningless it seemed to write "I" after having had this rather unpleasant experience. For me, "I" had now also become "he." Actually, I should start saying "we." I wrote "He writes," and the notebook writer also wrote "He writes." I write "We write" and the notebook writer also would write "I write 'We write.'" Who is this "he," in fact? Is it perhaps I myself? Or is it a mere word, without a name?

Whenever I recall that man of less than average height in the train speeding north, I feel disgusted. He no longer knew who was writing, so he gave it up—or perhaps I should describe that man as a writer who became unable to write. The man said that he left the act of writing entirely to "him." "I sometimes feel nostalgic for my mysterious rival. To him, I too was a rival, I think. I imagine him as even now writing fiction. But then I say to myself, No, that can't be. I have stopped writing, so how could he continue? Yes. It was 'we' who were doing the writing."

If there is one idea that obsesses me, it is, How can I stop writing? The account given by that man seems to me to be a kind of reply to that question. But whether the one who decided to stop writing, the one who thought he would leave the writing to "him," was that man whom I met on the train, or his rival—I can't tell. Besides, there are two or three points in the man's account that I find unconvincing. First of all, the fact that he is entirely too unconcerned about the body of the notebook writer, that is, his physical existence—or at least so he says. How could a man who was a young lover be unconcerned about the body of someone who must have been his rival in love? In that sense, his account seems too unnatural. And, if I may write a little about myself here, the appearance of such a rival is by no means a strange occurrence in any way peculiar to him, as he gravely assumed. I felt that such a thing might happen to anyone. In my case (and I can't really say why) notebooks are being sent to me. But you can get used to anything, even the strangest events. Did I myself ever have a physical interest in the person who sent me the notebooks, I ask myself. Apart from some considerable feelings of contempt and irritation . . .

What I hope for more than anything from the sender of the notebooks is actually that he, or rather, we (I had better say) would add a new word—even one would do—to the notebook. If we did, that word would become my own. Then, distancing itself from me, distancing itself infinitely, it would become our own.

I, or rather, we continue to dream of some new word written in the notebooks that are sent, and at the same time we dream of a universe in which the word itself will become a pure, organic thing.

And perhaps I ought to add that I promised to buy the encyclopedia that the man was selling. I have no interest in the population shifts in the cities of the world, but one must accord some value to the special nature of an encyclopedia: that all the various words and all the various things exist within a single book, having the same importance. At any rate, that's what "we" would seem to think. And since there is no one anywhere who can accurately gauge our numbers, instead of "rival," let us speak of "rivals."

Windows

He was talking about taking a photograph, a photograph that would contain within it all the fascination that the eternity of the instant holds—or perhaps I should say, he was talking about his dreams about such a photograph.

He thought about photographs almost without ceasing for even a moment, but—although his gaze always remained fixed upon the eternity of the instant—he did occasionally think of women. But he was not thinking of women in terms of what is commonly referred to as the incomprehensibility of their way of thinking and their physiology. Only when he became aware that women as physical existences were living within the eternity of the instant did he think of them—or it might be more accurate to say that he pursued his desire without thinking, and that was all he did with regard to women. Apart from that, he read books and ate meals and worked to get the money necessary for his meals and books and, at all costs, for pursuing his simple desire for women. But he didn't make money by taking photographs. He had rented out the small watch shop that his father had left him, and he himself worked as a phototypesetter. He made sure the watch shop and his own residence were clearly differentiated, creating a separate entrance for himself at the back. He worked three or four hours in front of the type fonts in the wooden floored room into which he had remodeled the traditional parlor, and would go off to the public bath in the afternoon, not only because he had long since turned his bathroom into a darkroom, but also because he liked the public bath. That was because he felt as if people's bodies were always about to melt away in the midst of the steam and hot water. He became one of those whose bodies were about to melt away. He was not the talkative type, yet sometimes he felt anxious if he did not speak with others. Sometimes he felt anxious about leaving his daydreams just as they were. He seemed to have a strong desire to turn them into words and tell them to other people at some point. He needed an objective listener to his daydreams, though why I was chosen as that listener is beyond me.

I was thinking about fiction and plants one afternoon in a tea room that induced a springtime drowsiness. It wasn't that the two subjects were directly connected. It wasn't that I was planning to write a piece of fiction about plants, but something else altogether. When I began to think about writing a story—it was a story with a very simple structure, but there were several problems to be re-solved before I began writing—plants got in the way of it. If you ask just how they got in the way, I can't clearly recall at this point; but the images of death and rebirth within plants grew up inside me like a forest and turned into pain at my being here, creating a painful sense of oppression. I tore apart a cigarette pack and wrote the following on the white inner surface with a ballpoint pen:

Is my gaze necessary for me to write about him? Is my existence as both narrator and at the same time recorder necessary to write that? Should I hide myself quietly behind him, and give him a name (a capital letter, or a very ordinary, realistic name?) and have him make his appearance as a character all of a sudden?

Then I thought about what kind of name I should give him, assuming he was to have a name; though I wouldn't actually include it in the story, I thought in as detailed a way as possible about a model chronology of the time he had lived through, which would serve to support the "empty portions" that would remain unwritten. He could only be written of in my novel as an abstract, allegorical being: for example, as one who "pursued his desires regarding women." But I wondered if he wouldn't be dissatisfied at being described that way. Might he not say that he was a different sort of person? If it were possible to do so, he might very well make some sort of mild objection: "The part you didn't write—I'm sure you realize this, of course, but what you wrote about was only one small part, and what you didn't write of was much, much larger. And I feel that I'm living my life within the flow of the time you didn't write about. Besides, you don't know anything about me, and I bet you never really cared about me at all . . ." That's how he might have spoken to me. "Do you intend to say that I, the character, am you yourself, the author?"

I was taken aback when he spoke to me that spring afternoon as the breeze blew into the tea room from the window. He seemed so serious as he said, quite suddenly, "Please listen to what I have to say." I of course had no idea of who he might be.

In the gloomy factory district to the west of T. Station, the army weapons depot was the only building left in what was otherwise a vacant lot. In my memory, it was not so much a building as a strange model consisting of walls surrounding nothing and a roof that was half fallen in. A model of what? To me it seemed a model of time. It was not such an old building; it probably dated from around the same time as the regimental buildings. But in those ruins there was what one might call the hum of a special kind of time that transcended actual, chronological time. The inner structure of the building was exposed by the fallen brickwork—the thick pillars, beams, and rafters, and the stone foundations. Windows were gouged out of the brick walls, which stood like a great double-paneled screen open at right angles to the south and east, and those windows had lost their metal shutters, becoming square, window-shaped holes revealing the empty sky. Windows do not exist as such in isolation from their surroundings, it seems to me; and it made me uneasy, as if I were about to be sucked into a time and space different from the space represented by the building and its windows. It was as if, from gaps in the physical structure occupying the space, I was seeing what lay beyond and could not normally be seen. Was it that I conceived, in my childish mind, the emptiness of spaces that ought to be filled, the darkness of the universe that comes when the image of the continuous progression of time is at an end?

The ruined arms depot was outside the circuit of my play-territory when I was a child, so it was only when I went to visit the family graves several times a year that I could go there, beyond the highway and the railroad line. The depot was surrounded by barbed wire and marked "No Trespassing," but judging from the bits of cloth and threads of various colors that were blowing in the wind as they hung from the tips of the steel barbs, it was obvious that the children of the neighborhood slipped through to play. It was this half-ruined model of time that I first chose as a "subject," so I remember it all very clearly. On short winter days, it would sometimes be completely dark when I returned from visiting the graves; and, at those times, through the windows in the wall standing with board-like erectness, one could see purplish clouds floating, blown by the wind, and the moon framing those clouds in a rosy light, and the twinkling evening star.

My first camera was a toy tin one of the old lens-shutter type that my father had given me for my seventh birthday, complete with a small spool of film and a developing set. The aperture was limited to either eight or eleven, and the view through the four millimeter-diameter finder looked like a scene from inside a small window with a rectangular black frame. At first I didn't know what I should take a photo of with that little camera; in fact, I thought it incredible that one could take a picture with that little box. Up until then I had never even had my picture taken, aside from the commemorative shots taken on school outings, and it was the first time I had ever held a camera in my hands. My father, wanting to explain to his son just what a photograph was, brought out an old album with a hemp cover and showed me several photos pasted onto the thick black mounting paper. Mixed in among the family photos of a young boy dressed in a sailor's suit and standing stiffly, eyes opened wide as if in surprise, against a painted backdrop of woods or European-style buildings as supplied by the photographic studio, and a little girl with a frightened look on her face, her hair in a braid hanging down in back, and wearing a kimono with long trailing sleeves, there were several snapshots about the size of a calling card. In these a young woman wearing a white blouse and dark skirt stood outdoors in the sunshine, stretching her arms back and leaning on a window frame. She had thrown her head back and was smiling at the photographer. Bathed in the bright reflected light from the white curtains in the half-open window and the sunbeams filtered through the leaves of a tree that did not appear in the photo itself, she smiled with great vitality. Light fell on her shoulders and on the gentle roundness of her breasts beneath the soft white sheen of her blouse, on the line of her neck, bent slightly back, and on her hair flowing down her back—all of this was captured in the photographs. My father explained that this was my mother before they married, in a photo taken by a younger cousin still in middle school. It was the first time I had seen a photo of my mother—or, more accurately, this single photograph was my first sight of my mother's face. Be that as it may, it was also my first experience as a child of an exceedingly strange and sorrowful loneliness. But what made me more uneasy was the light that enveloped this mother who no longer existed: the girl in this photo, bathed in light, was as yet unmarried, and had no thoughts of me, who was ultimately to become her son. Where had the light gone?

This is what photos are like, said my father. You should take pictures of whatever you feel like—it's very simple. And he showed me how to use that small lens-shutter camera. Take any photos you feel like, he had said; but I had as yet no idea of the connections among my own gaze, the body, the camera, and the images caught on film, so I was content for some time to simply hold in my hands the empty camera, with no film in it, and look through the finder. The scenes and objects carved into the shape of the little finder-window seemed to take on a special radiance. The finder was, in fact, dark and hard to look through, and since I had to keep one eye shut for a long time, the muscles on the left side of my face, being scrunched up in an unnatural way, developed a slight twitch and became quite stiff. Still, the world became brighter when viewed within the steady finder, exposing its clear outlines. Whenever that happened, I recalled the photos pasted on the black mounting paper in that album. This is what photos are like, my father had said, but he must have said it quite nonchalantly. He must have wanted to say only that a camera is a peculiar optical mechanism arranged so as to fix on photo-sensitive film simple objects, the world revealed by light. I knew my father and grandmother and grandfather, and had heard that they had once been children and, having lived several decades, became adults; but of course I did not understand that human beings live within a continuous process, within time. The image of time that charmed me consisted rather in the cutting off of the continuous process and its transformation into a tangible thing. On the outlines of the scaly skin that tightly covers such living beings as reptiles and coelacanths—. And my mother, though she was no longer here, continued eternally to smile, bathed in a light that moved in the wind within the photograph. She seemed to have kept on smiling from that static moment, in the direction of her future son, whom she did not know.

It was only much later that I came to think of photos as the eternity of the moment, but if you were to look for the origin of that idea, you could find its prototype in this single snapshot.

It took quite some time for me actually to press the shutter of the loaded camera and take a picture. My father said I should just take a picture of something, anything, I liked, but I didn't know what it was I should take a picture of, so my heart was heavy, since I knew the simple act of clicking the shutter to expose an object on film to be immensely important. By pressing a cylindrical, dull-silver-colored piece of metal about the size of an adzuki bean down by a few millimeters, one could peel away a sliver from the radiance of the world of matter and time, I thought.

Photographs suck out people's souls—not that my grandmother believed such things, but she often told me that people used to say things like that. Who cares about souls, anyway? Wasn't it simply that a part of the world had been peeled away, and made a stain there? A stain of light. In time I learned how to use the camera and came to understand what I wanted to take photos of. I wanted to photograph all kinds of things—the radiant silence of static things made manifest by a light that changes subtly with each passing instant, and my own gaze that was turned toward it. The blinding reflection of the too-strong rays of the sun sometimes wraps the reflecting object in a radiance that renders it invisible, and I will surely take a photo of that wound-like radiant emptiness. And of its opposite—darkness. The sea with its continuous cycle of ripples; the first gust of wind at dawn striking the highest leaves of the trees, and the way that is passed on and goes on widening like small waves; the curtain that moves in the wind like a pure white flame, setting its texture afire in transparency—whatever I saw, I needed to affix on film, as it was at the instant I saw it, the very life of that instant. In other words, I wanted to take all the instants of time that I was living and enwrap them in a thin layer of photographs—60 photos per minute, 3,600 photos per hour, 86,400 photos per day. And that thin layer of film, with its smooth, glistening sheen like a reptile's skin, is my very existence. I think of my world as an onion that, however much its skin may be peeled away, never weeps, and I give a little laugh. Yes—a world with no inner core. While seeming to be in pursuit of continuous time, seeming to constitute a continuous progression of time, each instant after instant remains static within the instantaneity of the eternal and, enveloped in the glory of things static, attains completion as a single photograph. It goes without saying that I have never considered such photographs "works of art."

In fact the first photo I tried to take was of the ruins of the army depot, but it was too big and would not fit into the finder of my toy camera. If I wanted to include it all, I would have needed to take it from far away; so, unable to take the photo from the angle and point of view I wanted, I had to be content with as much as would fit into the little finder. When the film was developed and the photo printed, the scene was completely different from the actual scene—or rather, from the scene I had viewed. In my vision it had had a definite sense of existence and clear outlines, but in the photo, everything was lost, transformed into a muddy, ash-colored lump, dreary and disordered.

Something is filtered out within the camera. I thought it was a phenomenon that occurred because colors were rendered into black and white, but of course that's not it. Something disordered, something we might even call the disorder of the world, is violently emphasized on the small flat surface of the photo. Things that do not in actuality seem disordered or unbalanced to me—no matter how unnatural they may appear, the things that exist in such disorder nonetheless have to be termed harmonious, simply by virtue of their being there—begin to reveal their distasteful, ugly shapes in the photo. I decided to choose objects that would be suitable to the finder of this little toy camera, suitable to the resolving power of this mechanism, but I also hoped to get hold of a better camera, one that I could operate as I chose. The next one I got was an old-fashioned bellows-camera with a fairly good lens; but it was still far from satisfactory.

Thus his story continued, but since what he wanted to photograph was limited to scenery (though I feel it's very inappropriate to call what he really wanted to photograph "scenery") no matter how long he talked, time didn't flow. It did flow very, very slowly, but he remained static in the midst of it. He finally succeeded in taking a photo of the arms depot ruins with a Leica that he got twenty years ago. Was it that this camera's sharp power of resolution matched, in part, his own vision? The boy who dreamed of enclosing each and every second within eternity decided to take one photograph of the ruins at the same time every day, from the same spot. He preferred the afternoon sunlight, so at a given time each afternoon he continued taking the same photograph each day for twenty years, never missing a single day. "And do you know what happened when I had accumulated thousands of photos taken over the years?" the man asked. One can take 7,305 photographs in twenty years, but one can't look at all 7,000 photographs at once. So, to allow himself to view all these photos at once, he transferred all 7,305 (there were leap years, don't forget!) onto movie film, just as they do in animation. The photos were apportioned into twenty-four shots per second, and the result was a five-minute short film. The ruins, eaten away at by time, gradually crumble away, but that process is too slow for the human eye to see. The casual observer would be almost completely unaware of the change, but still the process of destruction continues its advance, slowly, faintly. In the five-minute film, the ruins' walls are pulled down, down; and in the slow movement of time, they begin slowly, silently to melt away like whipped cream at room temperature. The rectangular window frames begin to melt, as in a dream. What, then, were those twenty years of compressed time? No one can say.

He wanted to go on and on taking photos of the ruins—in short, until he died—but before that, the building itself was torn down. He had been able to compress twenty years into five minutes, but still he felt that was too long.

Those twenty years of quite ascetical effort (a bit monomaniacal, even) had not been particularly hard on him. Pleasures like travel had been much restricted by this habit of his, but when it was all over, it was just a matter of the way things had been, no more. Even so, those five minutes seemed unbearably long to him. The photos that should have stripped from the world the eternity of each and every instant were, at 7,305, a very small number, hardly worth counting; so in that respect he had greatly compromised. On the other hand, he was dissatisfied that they could not all be crystallized into a single, unique frame. He dreamed of a single photograph that would be marked with a peculiar rarity as a pure stopping of the instants, cut off from the continuous progression of time: at once the sum total of the time of one's life and a fixed instant that had attained eternity. He couldn't attain to it, though, and he couldn't discover it in any other instant. He dreamed of that unique instant. Five minutes could not be termed "an instant," after all, he would say. It seemed, rather, like an eternity of time.

The Rose Tango

At my age, it only makes sense that I would think about the things that have influenced my unremarkable life. I have never formed the habit of thinking things through, so I have no idea of how to explain myself, what words to use. The year after the war ended, my grandfather, brandishing his old-fashioned political theories, declared that we were entering an "age of diplomacy," and made my younger brother and me take lessons in Chinese. It might have been good if I had really applied myself to studying languages when I was young. But since our world was completely buried in concrete material things—in fact it was the lack of any sense of fulfillment that impelled me to daydreams—there was no need to express anything in words.

How well, and in what succinct language, we would have been able to express everything that happened and even all we thought, when we were children! When night came, we would pretend to go off to our Chinese lesson, but would instead take the violin our late father had left us to an empty lot and practice there. We never even discussed the need to keep this activity secret. I don't know whether we had loved our dead father or not, but we had an unconditional attachment to the sweetly sentimental, high and clear cry of this violin, which we had heard long before. My brother and I hardly ever spoke, and this poverty of language, like all such conditions of poverty of language, signified innocence as against the ideas of punishment or unhappiness, or indeed any and all ideas. Our concerns were focused solely on concrete things; to be concerned with anything that did not have a concrete shape would be like having our souls stolen by the Devil and as sure a proof that old age was quietly creeping up on us as the appearance of wrinkles or gray hairs. We believed in the concrete sound of the violin. My brother didn't care to play it himself, so I was the one to play, and I did get better at it, thanks to my nightly practice. Then we went out into the night streets, pretending to be war-orphaned brothers, and made money playing the violin for drunken customers in bars. The drunks found us amusing and gave us drinks and tried to get us to smoke, and my brother and I accepted it all with a very serious air. I got very drunk and became unable to play the violin, but our business only lasted that one night, anyway. Some gangsters whose territory it was got hold of us, dumped water on our heads, took the violin, and chased us away. Our grandfather got the violin back for us later, but we got ten times the punishment from him that we had from the gangsters. Even so, we were still living in a world of contentment. In a world of contentment, like maggots or pieces of fruit.

My earliest memories are of Peking, where my father was the violinist in a group called Domingo Rodriguez and his Tango

Orchestra, which played in dance halls and places like that. We were renting part of a quiet Chinese-style house in the depths of a narrow hutong alley to the west of the Dong'an Market. The old corridors—with their stone floors and their scorpions—that faced the central courtyard and the courtyard itself were my playground. There were large jujube and peach trees in the courtyard, and in front of our rooms was a pink rose bush that Father had had sent for my mother from Shanghai by a German musician. That may have been our family's happiest time. Young as I was, I could not grasp what relations were like between my parents, but it may well have been that the assertions both made about the many sacrifices they'd endured in order to marry had brought unhappiness to the relationship. When he was not playing popular songs with wild melodies or tangos in some dance hall, my father was always drunk. It got so he stopped bringing home the money he'd earned, and Mother fell ill from worry. To get Father's salary directly from Domingo Rodriguez (a Russian Jew born in Qingdao, who was the band master and piano player), I would take my little brother by the hand and walk through the cold night streets of Wangfu-jing until we arrived at the hall in Dongtan where Father worked. "Domingo Rodriguez" was of course a stage name; he claimed to be Argentine, but in fact he had no clear idea of where Argentina even was. Rodriguez would hand over the money to us and say, with sleepy, half-closed eyes, "You poor, poor little kids. It can't be a happy life, what with Mickey's artistic temperament and his bitterness . . ." Perhaps he thought that Father went from having a brilliant future as a musician to playing in a two-bit tango orchestra overseas, all as a result of having married my mother. When he learned that we'd collected his salary from Rodriguez, Father would always slug me. But we had to go on living, even if it meant a beating. In December of 1945, the year we lost the war, my father fell down in the street, dead drunk as usual, and froze to death. I was ten.

In May of the next year my mother and brother and I were evacuated to Sasebo on a US Army LST tank-landing ship, and went to live at the home of my grandfather, who had taken refuge in T. City during the air raids. Grandfather was a judo expert, proud of the fact that he was a descendant of the Aizu samurai, who had remained loyal to the shogunate to the last. He had opposed our parents' marriage from the start, and Mother had had to elope to join Father. But it was a time when even our strong-willed mother could no longer insist upon her pride and on her right to have eloped to be with the man she loved. There was no one she could turn to but Grandfather. But that same year Mother passed away all too quickly, from a bad bout of flu, and Grandmother died soon afterward as well. Our family was poor, and since I didn't much like studying anyway, it was decided that I would go to work at a nearby men's clothing store as soon as I graduated from the middle school in our provincial city. At night, I practiced the violin by myself. It wasn't that I wanted to graduate from a music school, like Father, and become a professional violinist. It was just that the violin filled my heart with daydreams. Grandfather didn't approve of what I was doing, but the loss of first his daughter and then his wife had aged and weakened him, and he didn't express his opposition directly. At the men's store and on the streets I got to know some teenage hoods, or *chimpira*, as they were called, and became a member of their group. Most were kids like me: simple, "wild" guys from poor families, and without exception much less fortunate than other boys of the same age group. But when it came to their own fortune, good or ill, they were as unaware as a bunch of pearly maggots. We all had a deep-seated admiration for "manliness," but we'd never thought about what it really was. We used the word "manly" for everything beautiful whose surface had a kind of rough radiance. We were bewitched by rough, violent flesh giving off the scent of death, the flesh as life attired in the garment of "America," gleaming brightly like a movie on a screen. If I were to give an example of the "manliness" that we regarded as typical, it would have to be a young guy named N. He appeared like a whirlwind in the entertainment district that we hung around in, got into a fight at the Rhumba Tamba dance hall with the yakuza gangsters who controlled the district, and had no problem dealing with several of them all by himself. I still remember the Rhumba Tamba and the fight I saw there, my first ever. Tropical-style neon that bathed in a scarlet light the couples dancing among the yellow and green palm trees flashed at the entrance to the hall, and from the windows, with their gaudy rose-colored curtains of artificial silk, a constant stream of dance music flowed into the street. The red and green colors of the neon sign shed a soft light on the street, and we penniless *chimpira* hung out in front of the hall, showing off steps and wiggling our hips in time to the music. With vulgar words and gestures, we made fun of the couples who entered the dance hall, and puffed at our fags in proper delinquent style. We wore oversized, loud aloha shirts over bodies that hadn't seen the inside of a bathtub for a month, and our hair gleamed with pomade, which we firmly believed would drive the girls wild. Sometimes we were chased off by the dance-hall bouncers, but since we were happy and eager to run errands for the more influential gangsters of the district, once in a while one of those gangsters would take us to the dance hall and buy us a beer. One thing led to another and I found myself playing the violin with a small band that played exclusively for the Rhumba Tamba—maybe due to the feeling for music I'd inherited from my father. "Played exclusively for" may sound pretty impressive, but it was in fact a strange group of musicians gotten together in a hurry: two old guys—an accordion-player and a guitarist—who used to wander around the streets of the district playing for tips; a clarinet player whose day job was with a *chindonya* minstrel band that played at store openings and the like; and me on the violin. Our band name was the Rhumba Tamba All Stars. I felt I was now a real adult, and played that violin for all I was worth. I was called "Mickey," copying the name Father had used in Rodriguez's band. Since I had already lost my job at the men's clothing store (I wasn't even able to carry on a normal conversation with the customers), I was grateful for my new job. Besides, I really loved playing the violin—and not only the violin: I was drawn to all musical instruments. The members of the Rhumba Tamba All Stars taught me how to play each of their instruments; but it was guitar that I liked best, and I was really happy when I was finally able to get a used guitar at the neighborhood pawnshop.

Our band performed at the dance hall twice a night, from seven to eight and then from nine to ten, but I stayed on after we were done, listening to the music as it boomed out of the speakers at high volume. I never felt better than when I was listening to the music, shaking my body slightly to the rhythm. The melody and rhythm seemed to be pleasurably rubbing themselves against my skin all over, as if they were tangible things. They caressed me as though they were bodies in love with me. There weren't many dandyish customers who made a point of dancing the tango in prewar style; but once in a while the dance hall would play old prewar tango records by artists like Von Geczy, Leo Reisman, and the Orquesta Canaro, and then I would play my violin along with the recordings. The various melodies that I remembered from the performances of the Domingo Rodriguez Band would caress my body as if entreating me with their almost obscenely sweet and sentimental sounds. Then one night among those many nights, N. appeared and started to dance to Leo Reisman's "Rose Tango." There was an attractive if slightly overage dancer named Akemi who had drifted down from Tokyo. She was by far the best dancer among the girls at Rhumba Tamba, so when the young customer said he wanted someone to dance the tango with, she came right over and, with a supremely self-confident smile, took from his hand the set of pink tickets and put it deep inside the plunging neckline of her red "silk" dress. Awed by the aura of energy the two of them possessed, the other couples who had been dancing in the hall withdrew to the sidelines and watched them as they began to dance. The young man had the slim build of a pointer; his hair shone with pomade, and he was sharply dressed, all in black. He was the kind of man in whom dangerous cunning, coarseness, and a kind of intelligence, easily bred in poverty and ill luck, coexisted in the form of a fierce physical beauty. Not that I felt that at the time. I just sensed that the young man was the embodiment not of American jazz, but of the tango. There are all sorts of guys: jazz types, chanson types, pop song types, Hawaiian types. They all have an inborn affinity with one kind of music or another.

The two of them danced wonderfully together; but the man was rough, and by the time it was over, Akemi was breathing hard. The back and midriff of her red dress were wet with perspiration and appeared blackish, like clotted blood. This was not the night when the youth fought with the gangsters: it was a few days later, when he and Akemi were again dancing at Rhumba Tamba. The cause was jealousy on the part of the gangster who was Akemi's lover. Akemi had fallen head over heels for the handsome young tango dancer who had appeared so suddenly a few days before. Her lover was a gangster with considerable influence in the district, and he had brought three or four underlings with him. The world we are describing is extremely poor in language, and as a result abounds in the rich abstractness of violence and the flesh. Everything proceeded as in a pantomime or silent movie. As the gangster approached N. and Akemi, who were dancing across the floor, the last strains of the Rose Tango we were playing had just ended. One could hear the slight hum of conversation that always follows a number, the sound of the sky-colored fan revolving on the ceiling, and the heavy footsteps of the customers and the girls, who always walked in a weary-looking way when not actually dancing. When the big man in a white suit and loud aloha shirt approached the couple, he first grabbed Akemi's arm and pushed her against the wall, and then with narrowed eyes looked N. over from head to toe. Finally he fixed his eyes on N.'s with a sly upward glance and said, as if savoring the sound of each syllable, "So you're the one?" I could still feel the quiver of the violin strings on my fingers, and that feeling spread to my whole body, making me numb. The words "So you're the one?" meant both "You're Akemi's other guy, right?" and also "I'm Akemi's man. You mess with her and I find out about it, you won't be feeling so big. I'll have to teach you a lesson. Understand, buddy?" All of that was implied. At the words "So you're the one?" the underlings got ready for action, and the gangster's heavy fist hit hard against the solar plexus of the young man dressed in black. It was an everyday sight in this part of town: hoodlums in attack mode, giving loud, meaningless shouts and kicking away at a lone victim lying doubled up on the ground before them. But this time it was different. N. (though at this point I didn't yet know the young man's name) dodged the blow to his solar plexus with the speed and agility of an animal, and then gave a good strong counter-punch of his own. Shouts went up from the dance hall, and the accordion player growled in excitement, "He's like a bloody panther!" With the violin and bow gripped in my hands, I gazed—infatuated, unable to make a sound—at the body of the young man in motion. After N. had knocked five of his opponents to the floor, Akemi ran to him and clung proudly to his neck, but he freed himself from her hands and left the dance hall on his own. The manager of the hall, who had been cowering in a corner, rushed to put on a record, and the lively sounds of New Orleans jazz echoed though the hall. "Hurry up and dance!" he shouted to the dancers.

We young hoodlums didn't have enough money to buy alcoholic drinks, so we usually hung out in coffeehouses. Guys who didn't have enough money even for the coffeehouses would stand or crouch in front, waiting patiently for a friend to come by who might have enough money to treat them to a coffee (not that there was much chance of that). They chewed loudly on remnants of pieces of gum so old they had lost all flavor, and, like the men in cowboy movies, energetically spat the saliva that had collected in their mouths onto the pavement. The dry, dusty gray pavement was pockmarked with numerous blackish spots as a result. N. was the new hero of our juvenile group. Everyone was eager to be noticed by him; and when he walked by, we staged fights so as to attract his attention. Among all those young hoodlums, I was the only one who had actually witnessed his famous fight, so naturally the others demanded that I tell them all about what happened that night. They wanted a detailed, realistic account of it all, and they asked me for it repeatedly. And among the realistic descriptive details, lies began to creep in—the more realistic I tried to make my description, the more numerous the lies became. I told them about the pale, frightened faces of the onlookers, about N.'s eyes, tight with tension and cruel and bright as a jaguar's, and about his swift movements. I learned the rise and fall of my listener's reactions, and I learned that it was more effective to keep them in suspense when I told the most exciting parts. I racked my brains to make my description of N. leaving the dance hall as impressive as possible. At the moment that my violin was playing the last sharp, trembling notes of the Rose Tango, lengthening them out and then letting them die sorrowfully away, the door of the Rhumba Tamba opened, and the men came in. As the one piece of music ended, another began in low tones, as if in premonition of its first melodic line. In the midst of the dance hall's hum, there emerged the quiet, uncanny rhythm of the timpani: That was the effect I was aiming at in my narration. The seven-colored reflections from the mirror-ball, the brief exchange of words (just like in the movies), the large jackknife that Akemi's boyfriend took from his jacket pocket, and the way it was reflected in the mirror-ball (he hadn't in fact used a knife . . .), the way he held the knife, as only someone who had actually killed a person would know how to from personal experience, etcetera, etcetera—I described these things like one possessed. My psychology may have been similar to that of the *chimpira* who physically injure someone for the first time, or steal something—do something a little scary, in other words, and then, while still afraid of what they've done, advertise it in an exaggerated way. In short, my psychology may have been similar to what is called fiction. It's the weak person who turns talkative. Only, what I talked about was not myself, or the crimes I had committed—within the peculiar impulse that made me talk, there was something akin to a crime, something that could be termed misfortune. The act of talking, the loquacity itself, was the evidence of my misfortune.

It may be that I was in love, an unnatural love, with the young man called N., it occurred to me afterwards. When a taciturn person is suddenly transformed into a talkative one, there would seem to be some unnatural, irrational passion or unfortunate feeling being reflected.

Some time later, I got to talk with N. directly, but he'd learned of all my talk and said, "I never thought you were such a little blabbermouth," so naturally my sense of misfortune grew all the stronger. N., for his part, was an extremely quiet guy, and you couldn't begin to imagine what he was thinking. Akemi once told me, "He's a poet," as if she were imparting some secret, but that sounded as crazy to me as if she had said, "He's a woman." The last night I saw him in town he was terribly drunk. It was summer, but I was coming down with a cold, and, having finished my sets at Rhumba Tamba by ten, I was taking a shortcut through the mazelike alleys of the district in order to get home as soon as possible. N. called out to me and asked me to play him a vulgar tango, the sort with an obvious sentimental and voluptuous appeal. That was a good description of the "cosmopolitan" tangos that Domingo Rodriguez had played in Peking. I recalled as if in a bad dream the way my father's desperately roughened fingers performed these painfully suggestive laments.

"I can't play one!" I answered in a rude, ill-tempered way, my heart full of painful emotion. I had until that moment never thought of my father's music in that way. "Yeah, I guess it's too much to ask of a kid," N. said casually. Then, hard to believe though it may seem, he started talking about the poem he was thinking of writing.

"The ocean—a melting pot!" he cried out repeatedly. I thought that was the title of the poem, but he said it was "Universe and Time," a poem that consisted of the single line "The ocean—a melting pot!" He had cut away all the unnecessary, flabby words, the murky lard that thickly hid the essence of the poem. He had polished his work until all that was left was this one line. This one line, however, merged the whole universe and all of human existence, like an ocean, mixing them together chaotically at the fierce temperature of a melting pot. This single line itself, in fact, could not escape the defect common to all poetry—synonymous reiteration. That is, the ocean is indeed a melting pot, and this is the ultimate synonymous reiteration, said N. And his whole life would probably be devoted to writing a commentary, an immense commentary whose volume would be as great as the ocean, concerning this one-line poem of his. His life would probably end before he would be able to complete the work; but that didn't really matter because he had already, from the first, written the essence, the very pith and marrow of the thing. He intended to read every word that had been written about the sea, from children's stories to the most advanced scientific research. He would read everything, even worthless scraps of paper on which the word "the sea" was written in any language on earth, from Malagasy to ancient Phoenician. In this way, that single line would come to contain the whole globe. All words, all expressions would meld into one within the melting pot.

My longings for the hero N. were totally changed from that night on. N. had become no more than a troublesome, mad blabbermouth, who spouted meaningless nonsense. I promptly forgot about him, and never talked about his violent quarrel of that night, no matter who asked me to. And N. himself vanished from the district as suddenly as he had made his appearance.

Now I ask myself, what was N. to me? I hardly ever talk about myself or my family or my music. When I think about those things, I'm like someone who dreams but is not aware that he's dreaming: I'm not aware that I'm thinking. I have no need to speak, or for words to speak with. Yet with regard to N.—though I can't explain why—words and speech seem important. Nonetheless, in the end, all of these things will disappear into memory, and be turned into that strange silence that lies between memory and oblivion—the sounding silence of the sea of dreams—and go down to destruction together with my flesh.

The Time of One's Life

The images from his earliest memory always made him think of a dream. In many ways, he felt, they were like dreams.

He felt the same kind of vexing anxiety that one might when trying to recall a dream's hazy details. The first thing that came to mind was a dimly lit room. The room was enveloped in the kind of twilight one experiences in a dream or in the artificial light of a room underground, giving no hint as to a specific time of day. It was very clear to him that the room was on the second floor of the house where he had lived as a boy. He was able to recall several things about it: the dim radiance reflected from the slightly rounded corners of an old-fashioned radio, varnished a light brown, which was placed on top of a low, cream-colored chest of drawers, and the butterflies embroidered in white thread on a piece of Chinese pongee that rested on top of the chest. He had certainly seen such things in the room then. He had just woken up and was sitting in the room all by himself with his legs stretched out, wearing a white flannel sleeping robe.

This scene was his earliest memory, but whenever he recalled it, he was overcome by a painful sense of unreality. For "now," the actual time that he was remembering this scene, seemed anemic. He was no longer remembering; he was experiencing it. He had awakened, displeased and dissatisfied that the sweet fatigue of sleep was gradually fading away; he became "fretful," as parents often say of a young child, and began to sob, from feelings of anger, anxiety, and inexplicable sorrow. A weak resistance to that which was driving him from his sweet sleep. He lived through this again and again. Such times resembled daydreams, and were repeated so often that he became unable to tell whether they were actual memories, or the same dream repeated. Then he started to think that he had possibly been dreaming that time, when he was a little boy. There could have been a dream preceding his waking up, so filled with anxiety and sadness. It was strange, but it never stopped nagging at him—this idea that he was somehow required to remember a dream he had no real recollection of having.

Thinking that everyone must have such experiences, he sometimes expressed his feelings, but no one understood what he was talking about. How old would he have been . . . Certainly no more than six, since the first time he had recalled this memory was when he was six. He clearly remembered the odd feeling even now. He was taking a bath with his mother, who was washing his body and hair with the clove-scented, milky tea-colored English soap that his father always used. A steamy haze enveloped the bathroom in a warm, milky dimness, as he sat atop the wooden slats of the floor drain board with his legs stretched out. Suddenly he retrieved a memory from the tantalizingly vague ocean of time. The memory began to drift over the ocean of time like an anchor rope that had come loose. Until then he had never possessed a memory of that kind. Sometimes at dinner his father and mother would talk about the old times, before he was born. The names of towns in distant foreign lands he knew nothing of; the twists and turns of the gloomy lanes deep within such towns; the balcony facing on a large pond in a park; the seasons in unknown countries, and various strange trees and flowers—his parents left him out, exchanging the smiles of mutual understanding of those who have shared memories. He felt terribly unhappy and lost any desire to eat, astonished at the fact that *only he did not know.* "Why don't I know about that?" he asked, his voice quavering, on the verge of tears. His parents gazed at their little son in surprise, and his father said, "You weren't born yet." But the child stubbornly persisted, "Why wasn't I born yet?" leaving his parents at a loss as to how to reply. Then his mother gave a strangely sweet reply: "You were inside me, dear, and saw everything! Peeking out from my belly button—don't you remember?" He found this answer completely convincing, or pretended to. Of course this didn't solve the whole problem, since his mother also showed him a photo album covered in faded rose-colored cloth, and told him about the time when she was a very young girl. Once, the album was brought out when some people from his father's company were there. As he looked at the photograph of his mother wearing her wedding kimono and her white bridal veil, with her lips and cheeks rouged, he recalled being told how he had seen various things while he was still inside his mother. "Was I inside Mommy then, too?" he innocently asked, only to receive a harsh scolding from his parents, who were clearly embarrassed. From then on, he began to have memories of his own, in place of the delightful scenes he was supposed to have seen from inside his mother. He asked his mother while he was being given a bath whether she remembered when he had just awakened in his room on the second floor and had been sitting wearing his white flannel sleeping robe. She had laughed and said, "Remember? Why, I see it every day! What a funny child you are." "No, not that . . ." he began to say, but could find no words to explain. "I think it was when I was a baby." "Mommy remembers *everything* about when you were a baby. I remember things even you don't know about yourself." He thought that very strange, and fell silent. How could that be, he wondered.

It was the family custom to go to the movies together once a week, on Saturday afternoon, and he was wild about them. The lions, who showed the bright red inside of their mouths when they roared, and the horses and blue skies and ocean—all these mysteries appearing on the screen of the darkened movie theater as light and shadows of white and black thrilled him. When the circus came to a nearby park and he saw the feeble reality of a live lion (the fur at the base of its tail had fallen out from some skin disease) and the laziness that is the basic characteristic of a real lion, he was deeply disappointed. When he went into the theater from the street whose asphalt was melting in the strong afternoon sunlight—"the darkness of night was there, another darkness within the darkness, another night within the night, countless nights and days were there. After several days, or several years, or several centuries, he emerged into the street, dim in the long summer twilight, breathed into his lungs the sundry odors of the town mingled with the cool air, and felt the sensation of the still-warm asphalt through the rubber soles of his sneakers."

After learning how to read and write, he felt that what he was looking for was to be found in writings, and he experienced a mysterious happiness. In books could be found a world that did not vanish like a dream but appeared repeatedly, over and over, and so he "decided to place books rather than dreams at the top of the world's hierarchy." Since dreams were a "reality" that belonged too much to himself, they seemed less valuable to him, as is the case with all of our own possessions. What terrific dreams the kids in books can see! he thought. Unknown things and unimaginable things are crammed without limit into books, so it seemed that what was not written in some book most likely did not exist in the world, but there was no book that described the strange sensation he had regarding his oldest memory-image, and when he came across a book that he thought, based on what the adults said, might contain something like it, there appeared castles one could never hope to reach, and airplanes that could never take off no matter how long one waited—he was forbidden to read them, with the phrase, "when you become an adult." Then it happened that he formed the habit of reading books "in order to forget realities he did not want to think about." No one would tell him why (he thought it must have been because of some very unhappy experiences), but his mother threw herself into a gloomy castle moat filled with dark green water and died, and the following year, when he was eight, a young woman who they said was his new mother came to the house and began to live with them. His father demanded that he quickly forget about what ought to be forgotten, and nicely adapt himself to the reality of his new mother, but it was "the new reality, rather than his memories, that he did his best to forget."

When he was seventeen he underwent the "rite of passage to the adult world, a mixture of curiosity, vanity, timidity, desire, and pleasure" on a hot summer afternoon, at a love hotel by the river on the outskirts of town, with a woman twenty years his senior who had spoken to him at the movie theater. He felt "a slight distaste for the pleasure experienced with another's flesh as its object." In the dim light coming through the paper *shoji*, the woman put two cigarettes to her lips and lit them, then placed one to his lips: it was a gesture performed by the actress who played the heroine in the film they had just seen. He felt as if these acts held something that would fill the emptiness within him, and if he had had the chance he would have slept with numberless women without hesitation, "as when he learned to read and gave himself over to books"; but he always thought of himself as essentially an onanist. The reason was that he had an unshakeable dislike for any influence that his own body and his own fingers might have on women's bodies, in which many men take such great pleasure. The women's reactions always seemed to him superfluous.

When he was twenty-three, he wrote a story, but when he read it in a magazine, it had seemed inconceivable to him that he had written it. And it seemed still more inconceivable to him, "in the instant that he was writing," that he was writing it. He thought, Some other person is writing this. When, as the author, he was asked some question about the story, he replied quite seriously that he couldn't answer because it had not been written by him, so people thought he was both arrogant and a poseur.

Even so, in the ten years till he became thirty-three, he wrote enough stories to make up three collections as well as a volume of criticism, and all were published.

In the four years between the ages of twenty-nine and thirty-three, he wrote not a single story, only publishing in literary magazines a strange piece of writing that was a bit hysterical and incoherent. That piece began with the words "This will probably be the last of my writings to see print."

"The Time of One's Life" was the first of his writings that I can say I read. The text I have written above about him is a chronological restructuring of "The Time of One's Life." The author has repeatedly pointed out that "The Time of One's Life" is "not a story," but his insistence on this point certainly seems curious. Because if you are going to make a point of emphasizing that it is not a story, we begin to wonder simply if it wouldn't have been possible to write it in a different way. And to make a point of such insistence makes us suspicious. If it's really not a story, why is there a need to make such a point of insisting so? We'll say to ourselves that we are not such novices at reading that we'll believe it just because it's written that "This is not a story." We are all too familiar with the way of reading that reads the empty spaces and the words between the lines. That is almost as generally accepted as the way of reading in which the reader identifies with the characters in the story and with the narrator. It is even sometimes given the title "criticism."

We would doubtless be able to discover the empty spaces and words between the lines in his story and in "The Time of One's Life" without overstraining our resources; and we would also be able to label them dull works simply on the grounds that they lacked that kind of appeal. His writings are too abstract, and they are written in stock language lacking in concreteness (the egocentricity and stereotypical quality of the accounts of sex and of women), while his fixation with regard to his memories and images from childhood could be said to be just a familiar reworking of the self-identity gambit that forms the unchanging theme of literature. If one is lucky enough to discover one's self-identity, then I suppose one must be counted fortunate, even if it all seems a little foolish and silly to the onlooker.

In "The Time of One's Life" he writes that the story he was attempting to write represented "a childish wish for self-identity regarding a dream he had never seen, an infantile asking for the moon." Now he says that it represents "youthful passion" and that "anyone who is sane and healthy would be embarrassed to bother other people with such things." He cannot bear that people (especially young readers) should guard as the privilege of youth all these "youthful passions" that he finds "embarrassing." This attitude of theirs is nothing more than a passing phenomenon peculiar to literary youths and maidens who have read too many worthless novels, he screams hysterically, making us all shrink back.

At the age of twenty-nine, he married a woman. It was not that he thought that he could see the world with a woman like her; he married simply "because it was a perfectly ordinary thing to do in life." He had been an only child and, aware of the unnatural way that his character remained undeveloped as a result, he determined to have two or more children, and in fact did so.

And even now he must be living somewhere with his wife and children. I still have his three volumes of fiction and one volume of criticism on my bookshelf, and one can sometimes still find them in a corner in the local bookshop. I think of how the royalties from those books might be used for some trifling luxury to make daily life a little richer—extra income that permits the occasional dinner in a restaurant or a family trip—and find it a bit strange. It's not a question of good or bad; it's just that I am always forced to consider anew the fact that the things called "books" are always being converted into currency.

Ishikawa Jun writes in his essay on Mori Ogai and in "The Bright Moon Gem"—though the one is an essay and the other a story—about the instant when the 'I' in the two works saw an actual writer. The former gives us the experiences of a middle school student; in the latter we get a glimpse of a famous author through the eyes of a man whose house and possessions are lost to fire during the war. I am interested in the way authors appear to the eyes of others. This, of course, is not an interest in the personality of the writer, on the level of an essay on character or a journal of impressions of his or her personality. The author whose manifestation cannot be known except by reading the work—perhaps we may speak here of the substance of "the act of writing"—takes on a physical body and, either in the clear light of day or, as the title here indicates, by the light of the moon, appears as in a dream; at this, I feel a profound hesitancy that can only be termed terror. Thomas Hardy's story "An Imaginative Woman," for example, seems to have been written through terror of this sort, and most of Kafka's stories (though I may be charged with indulging in an overly schematic interpretation for saying so) seem filled with the alarming sense of witnessing the appearance of the author within oneself.

This is what he writes. From it, I gained the direct inspiration to write several stories. Or (and the idea makes me feel ill) the very thing I am now writing may still be under his influence. As if to make evident the depth of that influence—I learned of this only very recently, and it is most unpleasant and distasteful, but, believe it or not, after having moved about from apartment to apartment, I learn that Number 502, where I have been living since the end of last year, was his residence until ten years ago. The standardized layout of rooms in this type of apartment—at any rate the placement of furniture and bookshelves—tends to be the same no matter who is living there. Also, in the small room that I am now using there are a built-in desk and bookshelves that are just as they were back then (this is true of all the rooms throughout the apartment house); it is very convenient for me, but when I think that he wrote stories and "The Time of One's Life" at this desk—which, in fact, he did—it perplexes me. Isn't it just too strange?

Then, too, the concierge, who has been here for years, remembers him well, and seems to recall him whenever he sees me. Which is to say, the concierge, recalling the ways of the tenant from former years, applies to me the lifestyle of a fiction writer, which he has grasped from the standpoint of a concierge, with his superb professional sense. That's why, in this apartment house, letters that have been delivered in the morning and morning and evening editions of the newspaper are delivered by the concierge after nine o'clock at night, in my case only; with regard to the various regular inspections that need to be carried out in the morning (of the plumbing and the fire alarm and the security system), he makes allowances for me ("Well, as long as you're careful about things," he says); and the repainting of the balcony scheduled for all the units is specially—or I should say, so long as I am living here—postponed, since the concierge believes, by analogy, that my hours must be irregular. On the other hand, and here I really should thank him, on the analogical grounds that my income may also be irregular, nothing is said if I fall into arrears on my rent for as long as two months—and that's a real help.

He was unable to endure being himself forever and ever. As for me, will I be able to be myself forever and ever?

And now, at the end of this piece, I am tempted to try to make clear just who he was. The man who wrote enough stories and essays to make up three volumes of fiction and one of criticism, and who then stopped writing after "The Time of One's Life," is now writing, after a break of ten years.

Vague Departure

Just a few hours ago I gave up on my second departure—or rather, I made a total turn-around from the idea of departure—and, exhausted, returned to my room. After parting from the man in the tea room in the basement of the library, I became depressed at the thought that I would never have the chance to see her again, that she would never smile at me again, that I would never see the expression on her face again, and I walked distractedly around the park. I noticed for the first time that the life-sized model of a dinosaur skeleton that had formerly been exhibited in the garden of the museum had disappeared, and remembered how, a long time ago, I had gazed with the same sense of gloomy emptiness as now at the skeletal model of the dinosaur from the Cretaceous Period of a hundred and forty million years ago standing wet and forlorn in the ash-colored rain. I went into the museum's basement restaurant, dim and tomb-like, filled with the smells of mildew and dust, and I found myself among elementary-school students who had come on a school excursion and men of uncertain age with a look of semi-homelessness about them. I sat at a table facing the wall-mirror to the left of the entrance and drank a beer whose tepid bitterness was the sole stimulus to my tongue. On both edges of the discolored brown wooden frame around the dim, old-fashioned mirror was written in faded gold and red letters EBISU BEER; and on the top and bottom of the mirror frame was a similarly faded picture of the god Ebisu, smiling happily, carrying a large sea bream in his left arm and a fishing rod over his right shoulder, and wearing his trademark classical hat and garments. Almost thirty years have passed since I first saw this mirror in the museum restaurant, but it still hangs in the same spot, seeming steadfastly to refuse to change; and it occurred to me that the face reflected in it was the face of a man who, with gloomy resignation, accepted the fact that it remained his own. Would I, after twenty or thirty years had passed, be able to see in the mirror the face of an old man who was satisfied with his life? And would I remember, then? About today? Would I remember this moment when I was thinking, Would I remember? I thought hard about this.

I can't immediately remember how many years it has been since she left me. Trying to remember how many years ago it was—in other words, having begun to write as I am doing now, and noticing for the first time how time flowed within memory as well, I suspect that I began to be concerned about how many years ago it had happened. I had quite forgotten to think about how many years ago it was, and that amounted to having quite forgotten to think about how old I had been at the time. But my memories of her (though she had vanished from my sight) continued to have power over me for a long time, and she appeared in my dreams. If

I had a dream about waiting for a train departure while attempting to read a book among the elderly and unemployed who were killing time by reading a thousand kinds of daily papers in the reading room of the ruinous stone library in the park, I would think: This is a dream about her. Or I might have a dream about trying to find one particular book in a library that prides itself on its infinite collection. Then I would understand it as a dream about her, since all dreams resembled her, and spoke of her. And from time to time I was even able to see her figure in a dream. She may have had power over me, but wasn't I the one who had power over the dreams? Believing in the power of dreaming, I sought a sleep dyed in the twilight of dreams in order to live, but though I hoped to live as a being loved by her in my dreams, her form as revealed in those dreams was terribly vague and blurry in outline, and I always failed to realize that that vague form was hers until I woke up. In these dreams that were supposed to fill my emptiness, emptiness overflowed like a vague, indeterminate mist. I still could not forget her and, offering her my self-sacrificial feelings in those vain dreams, I became irritated at myself, and at the same time felt hatred for her, due to my hopeless humiliation. While clearly flirting in such a way as to enrapture any man, she allowed a meaningless, cynical smile to play around her lips—the privilege of a young and beautiful woman.

Her absence gave me the chance to gain the power to dream, and to entrust the power to dream to the fictiveness of words. In other words, for a certain period I may have resembled an author.

Rereading what I have written thus far, I feel surprise and embarrassment at what might be termed a tragic quality in the tone of my writing. I haven't had any dreams of her for a long time now, and have gradually forgotten about her in the endless continuity that is natural to time. So slowly that I never noticed, or perhaps I should say, at so natural a speed that I never noticed her memory grew distant, the way early morning dreams are forgotten upon awakening. And words began to live once more in the realm of actual gestures, facial expressions, movements, tones of voice, or perhaps silences. The women I had relationships with would demand that I say certain things when their physical passion was at its height, but, at such times, like any old-fashioned, egotistical man, I would reply with cold silence. Vis-à-vis men—my colleagues or superiors at work, or the very few who worked under me—I would repeat exactly what they said, although I didn't mind the trouble of changing the verbs a bit to achieve the proper formality. I had a hearty contempt for such things as freshness or originality.

I hoped that everything would continue on as it had been—my work in the government office, which I was not enthusiastic about, but which I had managed to do reasonably well, avoiding any calamitous mistakes; and the various little pleasures of the single man, about which I was more enthusiastic than about work: reading and afternoon naps in summer and strolls after supper, the cup of coffee I drank during the noon break, and the time I spent patiently waiting for a woman to stop talking and feel the urge to get into bed.

One time I suddenly noticed that I was not remembering her, and felt a mild surprise. I became cheerful, thinking of how well my forgetting was coming along, but then I realized that noticing that one has forgotten is a kind of portent that memories are coming back, and by way of violent reaction, fell into a sad, empty, depressive condition and spent an entire day off in bed, fearing a violent flood of dreams and words. When night came, I got on the subway and, intending to eat dinner somewhere, went for a walk, only to discover to my great surprise that I was walking along a street linked to memories of her, and that I had until then consciously avoided. I stopped in front of the house where she used to live (I had visited it many times, though I knew it would irritate her), and looked up at the window of the second floor where her room had been (how many times had I looked up at it, knowing that I was eternally excluded from the grace and favor of being allowed to enter that room). The graceful branches of a great old nettle tree covered in fresh green foliage half-hid the window; and on the gray tufa wall, its surface crumbling away, flowering raspberry and Scotch broom bloomed in profusion, as if the branches were festooned with flowers; their sweet, fragrant perfume, borne on the night's gentle breeze, penetrated the thin surface of my skin, and memories and dreams of numberless nights made my mind race with shuddering sensations a little like vertigo. I shivered and felt ill, as if with the onset of fever: I was remembering her clearly. The small, beautiful garden, invisible from where I stood, hidden as it was by the old building; the soft, fresh green leaves of hyacinths and daisies and pansies in the flower bed ringed with half-buried seashells, and the still softer-looking petals of these flowers; the pattern of the faded carpet in the small hexagonal parlor that jutted out into the garden; her shapely legs elegantly dangling from the sofa and swinging a little, as if in irritation; her lips, slightly twisted in a spiteful smile; her beautiful eyebrows, frowning in a look of nervous arrogance; the line of her white cheek, reflecting dancingly back the dappled sunlight that came through the window; my stolid silence and the inner ecstasy that made my temples throb when in her presence—I remembered it all. I would make up an excuse to visit her and sit there foolishly silent; meanwhile, she was cast aside by the man who was old enough to be her father. When, from a feeling of cruel despair and out of the need to insult the man who had abandoned her, she suggested we go on a trip together, her flesh, burning with inexpressible, violent lust, shone rose-colored through her thin white summer dress, so I passionately promised that, no matter what, I would be sure to meet her at the departure platform of the express train at the time she specified.

I can't explain just why I broke my promise. I've tried many times to find a word to express the reason. The unique word, such that no other words would do.

In the midst of the noise and crush of the rain-soaked train station, she stood wearing a light brown raincoat, her right leg crossed lightly over her left. The noise and humid atmosphere, overflowing with an energy that seemed somehow sad—the rapid chatter and convulsive laughter of the travelers and the people seeing them off, all a little jumpy or worked up through expectation or disappointment; the voice that announced the train departures and arrivals and that, though it had a curious kind of rise and fall to it, echoed flatly through the station; the screech of the wheels of the black steel baggage carts; the dull, heavy thud of cardboard boxes as they were tossed onto the concrete floor roughly but in a regular rhythm—all these made me nervous as I mingled with the crowds of passengers getting off the trains at the terminal and proceeding at an oddly slow pace toward the ticket barrier. I left the station by the park exit and walked toward the park, paved with asphalt and empty of people in the early morning hours. I walked aimlessly through the rain, making a single circuit of the gray, murky pond. Everything seemed somehow anemic in its grayish pallor. Gazing at the pond and the rain, which fell on the gray surface of the water and was sucked in, forming countless—no, an infinite number of ripples and wavelets, I was overcome with a feeling of terrible futility. Then, mingling with the homeless men from the park gazing blankly out the window as they sheltered from the rain in the shabby newspaper reading room that stretched like a narrow corridor on the third floor of the library, facing onto the inner garden, a room that seemed utterly forgotten and abandoned, I sat for a long time on a wooden bench and, from a window whose glass was broken (though in this dusty, forgotten place, long and narrow like a corridor, the majority of the windows had no glass at all) spent time watching great numbers of fat pigeons come flying in to strut, cooing, about the floor, and leave their droppings there. I didn't want to think about her, but fragmented thoughts of her continually came to mind. I could have been sitting beside her on the express train, anxiously wondering whether she might be regretting having come with me—she, looking out at dimly seen rivers and towns and fields distorted by the rain-spattered glass of the train windows, thinking of my slightly damp and humid love, looking tired and depressed, perhaps from lack of sleep, limply resting her head on the back of the seat. Then, as my body was shaken by the rhythm of the swiftly moving train, I could have watched the round raindrops on the window quietly begin to dissolve into question mark shapes and finally flow downwards, leaving streaks behind. I could have forgotten myself in the secret pleasure of daydreaming about her body and, drunk with excitement, gazed at that portion of it so full of life, like an ocean outpost where sea and sands mingle: starting from her soft, lovely cheeks, then suddenly shifting to her neck, elegant, yet with the firmness of a plaster bust.

All of these unrealized actions, gazes, anxieties, hopes, and pleasures filled up the empty time that had been magnified because of my unrealized actions. Running my right hand along the grand marble railing of the library staircase, I slowly descended and, crossing the rainy park, went to the underground restaurant in the museum. Drinking coffee that reminded me of reddish-brown melted mud, I stared at my own face reflected in the old mirror and wondered how she was.

I haven't seen her since then. I didn't have the courage for another meeting, and I was ashamed of my cowardly, mean-spirited betrayal. After some painful months had passed, I heard a rumor that she was engaged to be married, but it seemed impossible to find out if it was true or not.

Then, as I came to feel that it probably was true, I began to hope that she would forget my very existence.

At noon yesterday I got a long-distance call at the office from a man who identified himself as her husband. After a long, vague preamble to the effect that he was afraid it was very rude suddenly to call after so long a silence and yet under the circumstances he felt compelled to contact me, he told me that she was dying and wanted to see me. He asked me to come see her, if it was not too much trouble for me to travel so far. I felt strangely embarrassed and started to stammer, hardly able to get a word out as I listened to him.

I vacillated for some time, but eventually I decided to go and see her in the hospital. The thought that I would never be able to see her again plunged me into an intensely sentimental depression. She was dying.

Early this morning a man I do not know came to my room and said, "You cannot leave." When I was silent, he just repeated the same thing. He seemed a little embarrassed at the abruptness of his visit and, after hastily repeating the same words for the third time, his gaze downcast, he looked into my face as if at a loss what to do. He may have thought that he would find there some ready excuse for starting to speak, or some sign of permission to speak. And it seemed that such a sign did appear clearly on my face, for my early morning visitor came into the room, sat in my easy chair near the window, and, after letting out an odd breath that could have been either a sigh or a snort, said in an ingratiating tone, "You must have been all ready for your trip! When I was a boy, I was very fond of travelers' toiletry cases. My dad would check his Gillette traveler's set in its brown leather case the night before he'd go off on a business trip. He'd make sure the soap and the tube of toothpaste and the spare razor blades were all there. He was a very serious-minded man. The seven miniaturized items he needed for his toilet were all of gleaming silver, and shone like the idea of travel itself. They gleamed with a painful transparency, like scenery gazed at from the window of a speeding train, and made one feel somehow sad." Then the man actually did sigh.

"How old were you at the time?" I asked my visitor. Actually, I didn't know what to say to him and felt I had hit upon an inoffensive sort of question.

"I can't clearly remember how old I was. It wasn't a particularly significant memory, and I never bothered to ascertain my age while I was looking at my dad's travel set. Even now, I feel kind of sad when I see a silver travel set. So if you ask me about time—how old I was—I have no way to know."

That's how he answered me, so then I mentioned the doubts I'd had from the moment he came to my room. "Who are you, and why have you come here?" I asked, in an unpleasant voice. "And why do you say I can't leave here? Why, I'd be gone in a minute if you weren't here bothering me!"

"It's not a question of my bothering you or not bothering you—you can't leave!" said the man. "You can probably get to the station. But even so, the train you're planning on boarding won't be departing. There was an accident. There was a landslide in the mountains on the way to the place you want to reach, and all the trains have stopped, with no indication of when they'll start up again. If you like, we could go to the station now, just to make sure . . ."

The man might almost have been thought to be pitying me, yet he spoke in a challenging, malicious way. I felt very wounded, but I was aware of myself treating the appearance of this strange, talkative fellow as something quite natural, and that made me feel slightly ill. In short, it seemed like a dream. It was just like the kind of clichéd fiction that is developed in a dream. Then, as if to preserve my dignity and calm, I picked up the pack of cigarettes on the table with deliberate slowness, placed a cigarette that seemed smaller and thinner than usual between my lips, and lit it. I blew some smoke out (it sounded to me like a sigh), turned to the man, and told him I wished him to leave. I was aware of cherishing the fond hope that, by saying that aloud, I might bring to an end the dream that began with yesterday noon's phone call. The man left my room as suddenly as he had come.

After that, I picked up my piece of luggage, made sure I had inside my coat pocket the regular and special express tickets, blue-gray and pink-colored, in the little envelope provided by the travel bureau, folded up small the piece of paper from my office on which was written the location of the hospital, put it into the envelope with the tickets and went out, locking the door after me. I thought I would need to tell myself not to think about anything, but it seemed that my indecision, combined with feelings of despair that welled up in confused fragments, like foam on water, had reached the saturation point, and I could think of nothing. I tried to tell myself over and over that she was about to die and that she was calling for me, but I didn't understand what that meant.

When I got to the station, I discovered that what the man had said was true. Several energetic-looking middle aged men were listening to the announcements on the platform and complaining to one another: Could they wait on the platform for the resumption of service? Should they go by a different route (on a different line, then by bus and taxi to their destination)? And the railway personnel's attitude—it was far too bureaucratic, they thought, and launched a strong verbal attack.

It was announced several times that there would be a delay of more than four hours, so I went out to walk through the park. I was thinking while I walked, at this moment, she's lying there dying. It seemed unreal to me. A pleasant breeze bore the smell of tree sap, and the white blossoms of the slim, fragrant plum tree that was planted among the old chinquapins, nettle trees, and gingkos gave off a sweet smell in the uncertain morning light. In the front garden of the ruinous stone library, Japanese fern palms and magueys were bathed in light, appearing decorously characterless, like colored illustrations in some old encyclopedia. And so when the man emerged from the shade of the stand of magueys and fern palms, I didn't get such an odd impression, but I can't explain why I entered the gloomy tea room in the library basement with him. We drank coffee that smelled a little like straw spread on a cattle-shed floor (I gave up after one swallow) and sat facing each other for a long time in silence, on metal chairs covered with hard vinyl. As I visualized the newspaper reading room on the third floor and stared at the restaurant's shabby wall, trying to discover among its stains some sort of form, my decision not to leave on the journey gradually took shape. The thought of hearing her last words filled me with a wild terror, and I felt suffocated. Words like an empty, illusory flame. No matter what was said, or even if nothing whatsoever were said, I could not bear to be exposed to her gaze, or to look at her.

The mad, futile time flowed on, and at last I slowly went up the stairs leading from the library basement.

When tomorrow comes, or the day after, will I be able to wake up from this persistent dream? Will I be able once again to forget about her? Will I be able to run away from her words and her gaze (the sound and sight of which I had fled from) as they continue to spread in my dreams as an infinite dimness? It is not what we have done but what we haven't done that hangs suspended in irremediable time: Will I be able to run away from the knowledge that the words I refused to hear command me to repeat words on and on, without end?

Fiction

The platform was crowded with commuters boarding the 6:58 A.M. train for Tokyo and with high school boys in uniforms, their hair slicked back with pomade. As I passed a group of high school girls engaged in lively chatter as they climbed the stairs, the back of my hand was skinned by one of the blunt metal corners at the bottom of the heavy satchels they carried. The girl carrying it, intent on conversation with her friends, was swinging her young arms, her dark-blue vest tight around her torso, and her white blouse showing large perspiration stains under the arms. Off she went, unaware that the metal fitting on her satchel had injured the hand of a passerby.

A whitish, skinned area ran diagonally across the back of my hand. At its center was a red dotted line about four centimeters long with tiny globules of blood seeping out. Almost unconsciously, I brought the area to my mouth, licked it, and sucked out the blood. The minute quantity of blood had a slightly metallic, rusty taste, and I thought vaguely that there seemed to be enough iron in my system. Then, leaning against a pillar on Platform 3, I awaited the arrival of the train she would be on. Leaning against the pillar, I gazed at a road and fields beyond a barbed-wire fence whose stakes were painted with blackish-brown anticorrosive and several wooden billboards (advertising wedding dress rentals, obstetricians, optometrists, and electric refrigerators); at blue or red slate roofs; at white houses scattered over a building site that had been created by stripping away the greenery from the surrounding gently rolling hills and their slopes; at the clear blue sky of summer; and at the flora profusely growing along the tracks. The air was still rather cool, and the slightly sweet odor given off by the plants at dawn lingered. The summits of the hills were still veiled in a milk-colored mist, but the morning sunlight shining in from behind the hills and the wind were driving the mist away. Surely on such a morning she would come. Smiling, her mouth slightly twisted—from slight embarrassment and a kind of shame, her smile was, to use a cliché, masklike—nodding as she approached. That smiling look of embarrassment and shame that she always wore when we met for the first time on a given day made me remember the way she would lie in bed. Or perhaps it would be better to say not "remember," so much as feel her image race across my eyeballs like a sharp blade. Though surely she was not embarrassed at being so perfectly joined to a body other than her own. Her desire must simply be expressing itself in that way. She still hasn't come. From long habit, I began to think this way: She might never come. And that is, no doubt, why I long so much for her to come. Besides, she, or a woman like her, might never even exist at all. Every morning I would come to Platform 3 and stand for an hour or so as if waiting for someone, and then go home alone. The young station attendant would pass me with a peculiar, apprehensive little smile and start to water the flowers in their beds surrounded by decorative turbo and scallop shells, with a big tin watering can. There was no one on the platform now. I sat down on the sky-blue plastic bench and smoked a cigarette, gazing at the countless drops of water sparkling on the petals of the petunias and marigolds. Maybe I should have some flowers in my room, for her. There was a florist with many large greenhouses toward the coast, so I could get the flowers there. But if, in fact, she did not exist . . . I took just three puffs at my cigarette, tossed it aside and crushed it under my shoe, then got up from the bench and began slowly to go up the stairs. It was not too hot, and I might as well go home on foot. Along the coast there were several restaurants with large parking lots, and I could have breakfast at one of them. It would have tables on a balcony with a good view of the ocean—just what she'd like. What might she want to drink? Always, every time we met, she would order different drinks with funny names. She didn't worry about whether they went with the food or not; and anyway, she never even touched the drinks she ordered, with those ridiculous names. I would have breakfast at one of those twenty-four hour restaurants, a classy one, white, with a balcony, then go back into town and catch a movie. I had noticed the movie theater billboard from the bus I had taken to the station. There was a triple feature, all movies I'd seen two or three times already; but I always felt more comfortable with movies I'd seen several times than with a new, unknown film. That's the way children are, too. They're only interested in repetition of the same thing, in stories they know perfectly well. They won't get on a boat unless it's heading on a course that, though mysterious, is one they already know well. Though they're surrounded by so much that is unknown. *Peeping Tom* (I could model myself on the lonely, little forest creature-like cameraman) and Don Segal's *The Beguiled* and *The St. Valentine's Day Massacre* with Jason Robards in the part of Al Capone—a good lineup!

Then I went out of the dreary ticket gate, which had just been given its morning sprinkle of water, and started walking toward the seacoast. As I walked in the heat of the morning sun, I became very thirsty.

The restaurant I entered proved to be showy, with cheap, gaudy decorations and a balcony. Seeing yellow Guinness posters plastered on all the walls and windows, I ordered a Guinness and ham and eggs. There were few customers in the place, big as a gymnasium though it was—with just some well-tanned young guys and girls who seemed to have come for surfing or the like. Their raucous laughter and the clatter of dishes from the kitchen echoed from the high ceiling, and those sounds, which seemed somehow empty and forlorn, created the illusion of an autumn evening, with all the customers long gone. The space was air-conditioned, so the glass door to the balcony was closed tight, and since I couldn't have my meal outside, I decided to take the table closest to the glass door. By the time I had finished three bottles of Guinness and had begun to feel the need for something stronger, it was still just 8:30—it would be another two hours or so before the movie theater opened. If I started drinking one of the Cuba Libres or Bloody Marys listed on the menu placed atop the white damask tablecloth spattered with coffee and tomato sauce stains, I knew I would not feel like going to the movies. I gazed at the young girls, fawn-colored from the sun—the way they threw their heads back as they laughed, and the slight quivers of their backs, their breasts, their shoulders, all clearly revealed to my eyes. The girls noticed my gaze and made an effort to appear standoffish while their young sportsman-type companions, proudly childish, winked, bared their white teeth threateningly, and collapsed in fits of laughter. I turned away from the young people: I wasn't young anymore and wasn't suntanned, and, aware that I was an irresponsible hot-springs patient running from intimations of death from some vague illness, I felt miserable. Rays of the sun filtering through the pattern of the lace curtains made numerous small spots of light that flickered on the white ceiling, from which hung a cheap chandelier-style light fixture; and several of those spots of light made the facets of the chandelier's tear-shaped cut-glass ornaments give off a silvery radiance. With half-closed eyes, I looked at their reflections dancing on the tablecloth in a vague rainbow spectrum of colors. The tiny multicolored spots looked like insects with transparent wings flitting through a tropical forest after rainfall. Then I saw for a brief instant images of all the women I had passed up, or who had passed me up, fluttering as with wings made from sharp, transparent blades. Several indefinite shapes flickered in the depths of my eyes, giving off a white radiance; and several of the women's reactions—for example, their torsos quivering under my fingers—came to life again. How to name those bodies, how to name those quivering torsos? I had no idea whether they might be the body of the woman I was waiting for now—or rather, the woman I had been waiting for for so long.

There was still lots of time. It would be over two hours till the movie theater opened, and even if he watched all three movies, a long afternoon would follow: time when he'd be set adrift on his own under a sun which would never seem to go down. If he had some work to go back to, some work that made him burn with new passion and vitality (though to say simply "had" didn't seem right—he ought rather to have said "lived"), and if he were now on holiday to relieve the stress from that work, he'd be happy. He could be building up his energy, filling up on it, through this holiday. He'd lie in the gentle breeze and the sunlight, glistening fresh and golden, dozing the time away like a peach sweetly ripening—the energy of the flesh, abundant beneath the golden skin. Then there'd be the woman: a gentle mammal, whitely floating up, replete with rest and consolation and peace—a forest enclosed yet opening out, in the shape of an animal. When he thought of the times he had driven his desires to the point of lascivious ecstasy by treating the woman's body roughly, he found it ludicrous. He realized with some bitterness that his enthusiasm for such "ecstasy" was artificial. He felt hatred for those acts of his premised on the idea that the woman's body had within it some "forgetfulness function," or on the belief that violent physical movement bore the promise of being able to forget. Should he go back? It might be better to go back to his lodgings, mingle with the old people soaking in the hot springs, flip through the magazines piled beneath the table in the lobby, allow himself to be entrapped by some old fogey absurdly fond of talking, and be made to listen to a recital of the man's life history.

During the long afternoons, the hot-springs patients, waking from their afternoon naps, fed up with the tedium and lassitude of their monotonous, unchanging days, came to his room with expressions which, while drowsy and dreamy, were nonetheless serious. He realized that they were sincerely enthusiastic in their efforts to convey to him something about their lives. Among their numerous reminiscences and personal stories, there were always complaints and life lessons whose connections to reality seemed dubious; and this fatigued him. And if not that, then there were young men who'd come to the hot springs to rest and heal muscles injured in sporting events or work-related accidents. Since he was younger than the many elderly persons at the hot springs, these young men approached him with oddly friendly smiles. They rarely stayed as long as a week, and there was never more than one at a time. They would flash him an innocent smile and ask about amusing spots that might afford them some special pleasures. "There may be some, but I wouldn't know," he'd say, and a look of dissatisfaction would cloud their faces as they complained that they had no idea what to do with themselves in such a boring place.

To be sure, this boring, unstimulating life of his had gone on for more than a month now. If one took a bus to the hot springs nearer the coast, there were areas set up for pleasure, countless places of lewd liveliness with the humid atmosphere always found in such venues, scattering a bright, rose-colored light that was muffled in mist. But the place where he was staying was on the outskirts of town, deep in the hills, where only the true hot-springs patients tended to stay; and such patients were, in general, elderly. He passed his time there listening every day to the old people's stories—that, and going each morning by bus to the railway station to wait for her arrival.

It wasn't especially enjoyable, this listening business; it was more like a duty he needed to perform, although he couldn't say why. In his west-facing room overlooking a valley stream, he would take the teapot and teacups from their container, make tea to soothe the throats of his talkative guests, and listen as their everyday gossip, casually begun, shifted, as if by design, to an account of the speaker's life and times. These stories were vague in outline but concrete in detail: painfully dark accounts of lessons learned in the course of a long life, recounted with a kind of sweet objectivity. The old people never expressed opinions contrary to one another's. They agreed in acknowledging as right whatever any one of them said. He sincerely believed that the old people's simple words were trustworthy. In addition, he was very fond of the large mongrel (part hunting dog) and of the fat, brown, temperamental-looking tabby cat, both being raised in this prefabricated hotel, which was constructed on a modern steel framework from the new building material, plywood, and which could be called clean but cheap-looking. Occasionally he took the dog out for its evening stroll in place of the hotel owner. Unlike the owner, he utterly spoiled the dog, and it would feel free to run off, excitedly wagging its tail, and go down to the nearby stream to splash about in the water, playing to its heart's content and not coming home until nightfall (or, two or three times, not even until the next morning). But no one was concerned about the dog.

The hot springs; and the breeze blowing in from the sea, with its particles of light from the morning sun and its ozone; and the trees and thickets of grass, like green flames freshly blazing on the hills—all these would, it was said, revivify one through the restorative power of Nature. Several of the old people described these things in tanka and haiku written in peerlessly mediocre, formalistic language, or painted them in pale watercolors in small sketchbooks. That was the way these elderly persons expressed their deep emotions.

The old people had quickly decided that he was engaged in writing a novel, but there seemed something a bit unfair about the way they acted toward him. They kept after him about his occupation, but since he had always wanted to be something other than what he was, someone who would, if possible, not come to anyone's notice, he gave vague, noncommittal replies, and avoided saying exactly what he did. He suspected it was the work of a talkative female patient in early old age, highly curious and very much the maternal type: she must have done what she had often practiced vis-à-vis her own adolescent sons, going into their rooms and ferreting out from the contents of their desk drawers their innermost secrets (which were all related to a childish sexual curiosity about young girls, just as she had feared). And so she had entered his room, rummaged about in his belongings, and publicized the resultant findings. Once the rumor that he was a novelist was firmly established, some among the elderly patients would look at him in a manner that could be called serious, even modest, but seemed at the same time coquettish and patronizing, and suggest that he could, if he liked, write about them in his novel. Those who felt they had not been blessed with lives that were checkered enough to be "just like a novel" would still reveal what tales they could of unusual experiences or events witnessed—these stories were old favorites with which they had entertained their wives, children and friends many times, and they were told with the kind of refined skill that comes naturally from repeated performance.

He didn't know what to say to such attractive offers, and always gave an ambiguous, forbearing smile in return. His interlocutors would look somewhat anxious and perplexed (though it seemed to him they might be getting angry) and whisper, "Maybe my story isn't very interesting . . . ?" He would then have to shake his head quickly and assure them that it was. He felt he had by chance been turned into a swindler who gains nothing from his deceptions. He had been assigned the role of "novelist taking a break" and had to give the best performance he could. The hot springs patients didn't come right out and call him "the novelist" or "the writer"; but they tried to let him know that they knew what he really was through their meaningful glances and casually dropped phrases.

Though it was clearly a lie, there was even someone who insisted that he had read a story the man had written in some magazine or other. The rest were eager to hear about the contents and plot of that story; but, alas, the speaker answered, with a perplexed look, he had quite forgotten it. All this took place in the dining hall one day.

Were they, like the characters in Pirandello, in search of an author, he asked himself, while knowing that it was actually he himself who was in search of "an author."

After about a month of this quiet (or indolent) time had passed, a new client came for a long stay, occupying the room next to me.

The new man didn't seem to have stomach trouble, nor did he seem troubled with stubborn neuralgia or rheumatism; and there were no signs of a recent operation, with scars still red from healing over. After having met and exchanged polite greetings in the hotel lobby with its garish modern tables and sofas, and in the large bath hall and the dining hall, the new man came to my room carefully bearing a bottle of genuine cognac. There was only one glass alongside the silver-colored thermos bottle on my night table, so I got the toothbrush glass from atop my washstand. There were lip-shaped traces of white toothpowder on it, which I washed off, determined to have my guest use *this* glass.

My guest opened the bottle of cognac, poured it into the glass bearing the trademark of some beer or other, and tasted it. He grimaced and said, "This is good stuff!" We talked for a while about the weather and the scenery and the local geography—harmless topics that, however, were quickly exhausted, and then we fell silent. The bearer of the cognac silently downed several glasses in quick succession and, probably as a result, started becoming livelier, making several grandiose, mystifying remarks about the stream running through the valley outside the window (he claimed that the sound of the flowing water kept secretly echoing even in the depths of sleep, causing countless bad dreams about water to seep into his brain), or rather, about images of water in general. "Water is the bearer of death and madness"; "the sound of water is a silent language"—he said things like this in a curiously composed manner, not passionately, but in a high-pitched monotone. It made me uneasy and brought premonitions of something bad. He began to explain, through several examples, the image of the sound of water, or the sound of water flowing, as a silent language. Then he broke off and asked if he was boring me. I urged him to continue, out of a masochism filled with malice toward the speaker. I felt a kind of bitter happiness at the thought that there were plenty of people of this type. As for his talk, he seemed, despite his age, just like a student who, gesturing extravagantly at a water glass that has been sitting empty for over an hour on some gloomy coffeehouse table, tries excitedly to elucidate the difference between being and existence. But after a while, I changed my mind: my guest's words were as vague as they were clear, spoken by one who expresses by looks or by his whole weak body the scintillating talent of a born poet. Realizing this, I trembled with envy. Bitter as it was to admit, I was envious of those empty words, not understood even by the man who uttered them, those empty words that shone with a soft, rose-colored radiance. Words such as these, shining words bathed in a soft, rose-colored radiance, precisely because of their emptiness lusted after a shameless ecstasy of the sort one can only experience in dreams. And I thought, feeling a kind of despair, "Long ago my words, too, trembled violently in this shining, soft, rose-colored radiance."

That morning at dawn I awakened from a dream. I was conscious of having already been banished from the dream-state, even as I continued to taste the strange sweet feeling, numbly forlorn, as if I were thinking while still more than half in a dream-state. I remembered that I was weeping in the dream. I would let them fall—those sweet, comfortable tears, unaccompanied by painfully stifled sobs. Then I became vaguely aware of the pain deep inside my head, clearly the result of having drunk too much. Hadn't the conversation with the young man last night, too, been just a part of my dream? There had been another dream that preceded that one, and another before that, and in that endlessly, limitlessly continuing series of dreams—like Zeno's arrow, shot from the bow of an idea and moving with the swiftness of a dream—what if all the time in one's life could be taken up in dreaming, and one could awake from the dream to find that one was a totally different person . . . ? Or what if one were an actor in someone else's dream, a man you didn't know at all; and when he woke up, you disappeared . . . ?

In dreams you discover yourself tracing over the outlines, already written out somewhere, of all your actions to this point and all the words you have ever thought. All of these are written down in a huge book the size of an encyclopedia. Everything you remember is contained in that book, provided with a categorized index at the end and with signs indicating sources. You begin reading that book with extraordinary curiosity and fear, but at that very moment you realize that you yourself are the one writing it.

Then I fell asleep once more and awakened to the sound of water flowing in the valley stream. When I awoke, the first thing I heard was, as always, the sound of water, and I thought the sound was reverberating through the thin membrane between sleeping and waking. Almost as if it were the dull reverberation of my own blood circulating.

In the empty dining hall, I had a quick breakfast of black tea and cold eggs while listening to the sound of the women washing the dishes; then, in keeping with my usual custom, I went down the hill to the bus stop and got on a bus bound for the railway station.

He noticed with puzzlement that he was seeing the train station, square and painted cream and dark brown, for the first time. He had never given any thought before to what kind of building it was. On Platform 3, deserted now and casting its shadows in the morning sun, he waited for the train to arrive. At last it slid into the platform, its wheels screeching against the rails, the automatic doors opened with a loud sigh, and a woman—a woman wearing a white linen traveling dress that clung tightly to her body—stepped down onto the platform, which, obstructed by the train, lay in shadow. First he saw her feet encased in slim black sandals and the white skirt that swayed slightly as she walked; then her hips, her breast, her neck, and her smiling face. He could tell that her smile was directed at him, and he gazed into her face. Was this, this woman, the one he had been waiting for? After the train, which had stopped for a while, left the platform, the woman floated up in the brilliant, transparent radiance falling there, and its flames, reflected against her white linen clothing, seemed to tear away what she was wearing to reveal her naked body. He had no idea of what words to use to address her. He didn't even know her name. "Who is she?" he thought. "Surely this is a scene I've read about somewhere. Or written about . . ."

The Voice

"Why was I drawn to the momentary sound of wings,
more fleeting even than the moth itself?"
In dreams of another
"So long as you live, you keep on aging"
—from Yoshioka Minoru, "Water Mirror"

Ten or more years ago I was told by older friends about ideas for
a great many novels that probably remained unwritten in the end.
They resembled confessions of the secrets of someone's parentage,
or whispered confidences regarding love affairs that would create difficulties for "the other man's wife" if revealed. And certainly
there were among them ideas like as-yet unpolished gems that
would yield impressive short stories if handled with talent and the
technique that comes with long years of experience. Why, then,
did they not write them? I cannot, however, deny my own slightly
perverse sense of triumph at their not having written them. This
wicked sense of triumph regarding those who attempted to write
but could not was something that often filled me with rapture.

To put it clearly, I held them in contempt. It was not simply that I disliked the literary obsessions that their attitudes, the look in their eyes, and the words they spoke so naturally revealed; I in fact could not endure them. Why shouldn't these writers come to grief? I took an aggressive stance, and mocked the ideas for the stories they were trying to write and their innocent literary obsessions. Even now I can recall with feelings of regret several scenes like that, but (as the sensitive reader will have understood already and hence there is really no need to write it here) I too had ideas (childish ones) for a story I was trying to write, and innocent literary obsessions of my own. In short, they and I—though I would never have admitted it at the time—resembled one another.

At an exhibition of my sister's works, I met one of the writers after a gap of ten years or more. Out of a peculiar sense of shame, I put on a show of surprise and, as one always does in situations like this, asked what he had been doing, without feeling much interest in his answers, and urged him to have some chocolates and domestic brandy. It would be a bore for me to describe what the years had done to him: this chubby man nearing forty, looking like a bank clerk, and apparently full of confidence—of the sort that any sensitive observer could tell at a glance was just a show; writing about such a middle-aged man is just plain boring. He had come late in the afternoon and sat sipping away at the brandy until the gallery was about to close. In the end he succeeded in making us invite him for dinner. In the old days, too, he had always managed to extend his stays until dinnertime in precisely the same manner. Of course my sister and I invited him in such a way as to suggest that we assumed he would refuse; if he did not notice our tone, it could only be because he chose to ignore it. The conversation tended to lapse, but when our depressing, indigestible meal had at last reached the point of after-dinner coffee, he started to explain the reason for his sudden visit. He began casually with a critique of my stories that mingled purposeful flattery with what amounted to highly malicious judgments, and then seemed content to pursue the rest of the conversation at his own sweet pace. He had completed a novel on a theme he had been mulling over for the past ten years ("I've discussed it with you before, so I'm sure you remember"). He had decided to cut the somewhat verbose, gorgeous purple passages that constituted not only the beauty of his style but also its weakness (on the analogy of a two-edged sword). He had substituted a strong, sharp, and simple style. This was said with a face that gleamed with excitement, and with a drunkenness resulting from the wine and brandy he had been lapping up: "As you probably know, my novel's theme is the trinity of metaphysics and common melodrama and theoretical physics." Looking pleased as could be with himself, he put his elbows on the table and then clasped his hands and rubbed them together, while favoring us with a magnanimous smile. After pausing for breath, he pressed forward with his speech—and this was his real object. A certain small publisher had indicated that they might be willing to publish this novel of his (of over three thousand manuscript pages), and one more push should do it. And to make that last push as strong as possible, to lend his novel decisive added value, he would like to have Haniya Yutaka write the epilogue—though he himself didn't really like having to ride on the coattails of an established writer, he averred. Then he moved to checkmate me: "Introduce me to him." I said by way of reply that I didn't personally know Mr. Haniya, or authors of his stature, and that I hadn't even read his books. He looked disappointed and humiliated, but still managed to name several other famous authors. Upon learning that I knew none of them personally, he looked dumbfounded and fell silent. Seeing how disappointed he was, I actually began to feel somewhat apologetic toward him.

For some time afterward, I lived in fear of his telephone call. Fortunately I didn't know any of the writers whose names he'd mentioned that day, but he might always call and ask me to introduce some other writer whose name had occurred to him: What a depressing thought! Even if I refused, I would of course have to listen to his talk, and that was a gloomy prospect in itself. My anxiety was only increased by the comments of my sister, who enjoyed making predictions about how badly things tended to turn out. "That megalomaniac, with his old-fashioned literary theories," she said, "he'll be sure to call again and demand an introduction to some impossible author. And no doubt he'll be sending along a package with his novel of over three thousand pages, too."

In time, though, I forgot all about the matter, and lost myself in the ordinary events of everyday life, like taking walks, seeing movies, talking with friends, knitting things for winter, and reading in bed. I recalled how, several years ago at some literary meeting or other, I was abruptly asked by a woman writer who had spent many years abroad, "Do you enjoy your daily life?" I had never thought about such a thing—whether my daily life was enjoyable or not—so I didn't know how to answer at the time. But now the dreaded phone call did not come, and there was no package containing a novel of over three thousand pages in the mail, so it occurred to me that, yes, my daily life was enjoyable. Besides, I had no dramatic past to write about, so there was no reason for me to become the object of revenge from someone from that past or to be afraid of hearing his voice. Thus, I really had the right not to think about whether my daily life was enjoyable or not. This may be a decisive weak point for a "novelist," or a lack that renders the novelist's very existence doubtful; but even if that were so, what in the world could I do about it? If I didn't write stories, some other existent self—another me, to put it plainly—would continue to do so. And I felt that it wouldn't matter if it wasn't even "another me" after all. Indeed, it could all be left to the countless beings in those places where the reference to "myself" had lost all meaning. I felt that was so with a happiness that was almost carnal. A painting of a large tiger that I saw at an exhibition somewhere made me feel uneasy, but I am not a character in a novel by Huysmans who falls into madness from gazing too long at a painting. It was a painting in which the stripe-like clouds that blaze up in the sky behind the tiger, with its somehow childlike ferocious countenance, seem identical to the tiger's stripes, so that the mirror of the sky seems to be reflecting only the stripes of the tiger. It reminded me of the following passage from a story by Borges: The painting "had stripes like those of a tiger, and seemed to be shouldering a silent, recumbent one." In the symmetry between the tiger and the striped sky, there is a solitary madness that marches steadily onward—not that there could be a madness that is not solitary—and it was that that made me uneasy.

But of course I was not thinking only of the painting of the tiger. If the tiger with the formalized stripes symmetrical with the clouds in the sky should actually appear in my dreams, that would seem to suggest some degree of madness. But in my dreams there appeared only a huge cat, a cat with stripes—perhaps a vulgarized version of a tiger—that, over and over, leapt gracefully in from my bedroom window.

When I thought about it, I realized that the voice was not unlike the cat in my dreams that kept bounding in through the window, again and again.

I hardly know what to call that voice, or how to name it.

It invaded via a machine that suddenly began to ring shrilly. The voice didn't say who it was, and when I asked, it replied, with a peculiar dry laugh that seemed to come from far away, "There's hardly any point in giving you my name." Then it would ask repeatedly whether the person now on the phone "was really the author Miss Kanai, or not?"—this in an urgent tone, with a little quaver at the end of some words. She hung on stubbornly: "You're really the one that wrote that novel? That disgusting novel?" I felt no need to respond to such meaningless, relentless, and even underhanded-sounding questions (and asked in such an unmannerly way, by a voice I didn't recognize); but still I didn't hang up, out of the masochistic, self-challenging feeling which everyone has at times: the sense that one should choose to confront something unpleasant, even though it would be just as easy to evade it. While feeling an irritated disgust at the unnaturalness, or rather, the unreality of identifying myself in such circumstances, I answered briefly

"Yes," in an unpleasant, harsh voice, as if uninterested, and taking pains to sound cold. But the other party asked the same question over and over, the voice gradually becoming shriller, and with a disturbing tone that sounded like a weak, childish cry. I found it quite impossible to say, "I am the novelist Kanai Mieko"; but I felt that the voice was trying to get me to say precisely those words. It would be unnatural to do so, and would sound to my own ears like an outright lie. When this telephone call came so suddenly (though of course telephone calls always come suddenly), I was reading the poems of Yoshioka Minoru in the November issue of *Literary Arts*; it must have been a little after ten at night. The poem "Water Mirror" made a special impression on me. However, I had heard, one afternoon a few weeks before, while having a cup of tea on my way back from the funeral of Miyakawa Jun ("I don't want to write about a living author," he used to say: a contempt for the body that itself gave off a certain odor of mortality . . .) that Yoshioka Minoru had used certain phrases of mine in a poem he had recently written. I knew, of course, that poets write their poems by inlaying (or interweaving) the words of others, and I had read Yoshioka's poem with a kind of thrilled interest. The words quoted in brackets in the poem were ones that I had once written—yet that fact seemed lacking in reality, which made me feel somehow free, liberated. To put it more simply, I experienced an infinitely sweet joy at those words being set free from the spell that intones "I have written this." I had the sense that there was no need to test the flavor of those words; that the meanings I had tried to give them had vanished; that the words came before me as naked objects, purified anew.

Those words say, for example:

A night when water drips from the ceiling
Washing the frying pan, I think
"It's through our gazes
rather than our bodies
That we come together."

It is of course meaningless to wonder who wrote these words.
The voice filtered through the telephone had an unreal quality, a metallic unreality; if I were lucky enough to have a need to confess my love for someone (or if I had any impulse to, perhaps I should say), I would not hesitate to use the telephone to do so. I would not hesitate to use the telephone, though no doubt there would be vacillation regarding the confession itself: Confessions are always impulsive. That voice was surely a meaningless confession, an impulse resulting from the exhaustion of vacillation. I had been spared the arrival of a package containing a long novel in excess of three thousand pages, a literary trinity of metaphysics, vulgar melodrama, and theoretical physics; instead, I had to listen to the voice of someone, apparently a young girl, who called herself my "reader." In any case, it came in my direction from beyond time.

That voice, the voice (or rather, the tone) that was now connected to me by telephone asked again and again, with a quaver at the end of every phrase, and in a tense way that made me very uneasy, if I was in fact the author Miss Kanai. "Really? Is this really the author? Truly?" And because of that voice, I became troubled with a strange sense of unreality. All the various subtle tones of that voice seemed to infect me, as if with a communicable and incurable disease; the process seemed to deplete me. When, out of distaste and dislike, I tried to hang up the phone, she would moan, "Do you hate talking to me so much, then?" I had the illusion that I had turned into a man who had cruelly betrayed some girl. On one and the same night, there were seven calls in that same voice. Sometimes one feels a wicked joy at discovering in someone else a kind of pointless madness, undefined, undeveloped as an unhatched egg. Also, and I say this without a bias of any kind, madness invites laughter, despite the surrounding tragedy. People are roused to laughter at madness—due to an essential grotesqueness that cannot be explained away by such psychological motivations as the need to distract oneself from feelings of shame or anxiety.

And so there was something grotesque about that voice on the telephone. Something like a sad grotesqueness, a heart-wringing, serious grotesqueness that tries to read reality through fictional words.

Could it have been "from my heart," or "from my world of ideas"? Was it "for certain, my shadow, my echo"? Really? Is there really a wilderness within me? I wrote that "I have no dramatic past to write about," and that is true; and yet the works that I've written help create the "present" of persons unknown to me. The voice on the phone drawled confused, pointless words, as if to itself, and kept repeating that I had stolen her future. The man who had completed his three-thousand page novel (he had been, though not a friend, at least an acquaintance) said with a rancor tinged with sadness when he left that night, "You've written about me in your stories endless times, and have appropriated my past." Pretending not to have heard, I smiled magnanimously, like a true writer, and said as seriously as I could, "If I can be of any help to you regarding your novel, don't hesitate to call on me." (Most men die leaving behind only "monologues" and "fragments.")

"How could I steal your future?" That's how I replied to her. "How can you say such self-centered things?" she then said. "Don't you feel sorry for me at all? I don't have much money, you know, but I went out and bought your book with my own money—my own money! And I bought magazines with your stories in them, too. And I read them all, I did! When I read page twenty-six of *The Sea Without a Shore*, I just felt like dying. Yet here you are talking in that conceited old woman's voice of yours—and you're fat, too, judging from that cover photo on *The Acacia Knights*! I wanted to write novels too, you know. But never mind. I'm not leading a well-regulated, ascetic sort of life, like the characters in your books; and I'm sure you despise people who've gone astray. I was so lonesome I just had to have a little drink a while ago. [Sobs. Thereafter, spoken through her tears.] I—I'm only twelve, and here I am, destroying myself with drinking! And, I'm currently reading page twenty-six of *The Sea Without a Shore*."

The next day, I was irresistibly tempted to see what I had written on page twenty-six of my novel—which of course I could hardly be expected to remember. (Usually I want to forget all about something I have written once it appears in book form.) This is how page twenty-six begins:

It is no doubt true that I am no longer a child. Certainly I am, in a sense, no longer very young. I know that by looking at myself. My skin doesn't contain as much moisture or oil as it once did, and even my blood is less plentiful! Moisture and oil—now those are what make you young. Like milk and honey, they're images of abundance. And this is true, an unmistakable fact, the reality of my life. To put it plainly, I've aged. Coming back to this house, coming back to the house where I was born and raised, I discovered this. There was no way I could go on living pleasantly and freely now. The entire house was telling me that. This house in which no one from my family still lived, this house that was the port from which I had first set sail.

What boring writing this is! This may smack of self-congratulation, but it seems to me that even I wrote passages a bit better than this in that novel.

Two or three days later, there was another phone call from that voice. This time she claimed that she had written *The Sea Without a Shore*. "I'm not saying you stole it. It wouldn't be strange if the same novel was written at almost the same time by somebody else—or by any number of people, even—who didn't know about the other writer," she explained.

The day after this call there was yet another from her. "What I said yesterday—I'm sure you understand this already—well, it was, as you can imagine, actually the idea for a novel I'm going to write." This was said in a gloomy voice. "Its title will be *The Sea Without a Shore*," she said with a triumphant laugh.

And there was another call from her.

"Since you are such a bold, shameless, cruel person, I'm sure you intend to put me into a story of yours. Why, this'll be good material for a novel, you say to yourself, and probably take notes on my calls—you might even be recording them. You'll title it *The Voice*, and describe me as 'my shadow, my echo . . . come from my world of ideas,' quoting Yukio Mishima's 'From the Wilderness.' Right on target, aren't I? Never mind. Go ahead and write it."

And so I wrote this. Contrary to her assertion, I didn't make notes or record her calls; but most of what she said was true. Or, to put it more exactly, one part was true. I wonder if she'll read this, this story that I'm now writing? "Why do you write stories?" she asked. "Tell me the truth." The truth! Why do "they" always want to know the truth?

To tell the truth, I would like to have spent my whole life as a reader. Of course, I am a reader with regard to everything that I did not actually write; but sometimes I wish that I could have been a reader without this limitation: a reader with no claim to having written anything at all. Not a reader like *Madame Bovary* or *Don Quixote*; one would have to be the sort of reader who lives her whole life only for the modest pleasures of reading, who fortunately makes no missteps. I feel that someday it will be possible for me to become someone like that. Or will I keep on starting to write new things, like the peach in my solitary dream: "One spring day, within the fruit of a yellow peach that had put forth its pink blossoms, sweet nectar welled up, dripping with ripeness"? Writing again and again, even while trembling at the words I have written? Words that may become enervated in an extremely individual kind of intimacy, like the fruit of the peach, which begins gradually to rot from the very place against which one's finger has firmly pressed—

The curious illusion that I may still have something to write about seems to keep me bound to the act of writing. Will this curious illusion at some point reveal its cruel, true form? I have no desire to chew over with still more bitterness the bitter aftertaste of my critical writings, which can justly be described as circuitous baby talk, or the stories and poetry I have written up to now (I myself acknowledge these to be very badly done, or rather, more than badly done; they amount to nothing more than everlasting fragments). They seem so slight, even as the bitter aftertaste that is all that remains to an author who—perhaps without really wanting to—has written something. Also—and this is the most important thing—it seems inconceivable to me that it was I who wrote those works, however slight and badly done they are. There was a poet who wrote of his own works, "Did I write this?" And Jonathan Swift, lying ill in old age and having *Gulliver's Travels* read to him, also asked, "Did I write this?" I am not, of course, placing the "works" that I have written on the same plane as *Gulliver's Travels* or the works of that poet, who possessed an unquestionable talent all his own. I am only speaking of the strange relationship between a writer and his or her works.

I would like to be as disconnected as possible from the works I have written (and the very word "works" is itself an ambiguous and provisional way of referring to them). That's what occurs to me as I wash the frying pan on a night when water drips from the ceiling. And, with reference to the words I have written, while being resigned to the fact that I have indeed written them, I feel an almost blind impulse in the presence of others to maintain the impression (a bit forced, to be sure) of having forgotten about them entirely. This seems to be an uncontrollable reaction on my part, virtually identical to the sweat that forms in one's armpits (a part of one's body swathed in clothing) or the more readily apparent flush on one's cheeks (the blood blazing up just beneath the skin and suddenly visible)—physical phenomena that occur (regardless of whether others happen to notice them or not) when, trying to keep something hidden, one tells a lie. And so, "I gaze from an awkward spot at a bare winter tree in silhouette."

The Moon

According to Mother, I was already old enough to go on errands all by myself, even at night. "The chicken butcher and the green-grocer just in front of it, near the castle at the edge of the shopping area, should be open till nine, and I want you to get me a chicken and a package of mushrooms there. I'm sorry you have to go at night like this, but I can't go right now. You know that, don't you, dear?" Of course I couldn't say no. "Your older sister"—she had died at age six—"used to take a little wicker basket and go buy the enriched powdered milk she always drank," Father said, laughing good-naturedly; but Mother looked a bit sad. Then I went out into the town, where the last dim twilight had been swallowed up in night.

It was late at night when the express train reached the town. I was surprised to see that the hotel in front of the station, where I'd made a reservation, looked completely different from before, having been transformed into a brand-new, eight-story, gray building. But I should have foreseen it, since I could hardly expect the express train to arrive at exactly the same city it had been ten years before, except perhaps in a dream. I have the impression that I had been seeing a great number of short, fragmentary dreams more or less continuously from the time I was on the train, but when I woke up in the morning at the hotel, I couldn't remember a thing. I felt depressed and disgusted. I tried to recall the love I had once had for the dead woman, but nothing came. The only things I clearly remembered were that I had hated her husband and that she was always humiliating me; yet even those details were somehow ambiguous, with little sense of reality. When I tried to think of her, all that came back were several fragmentary, unclear memories, lacking in any vivid or deep feelings; so I felt that the love I had had for her for so long also lacked reality. But even so, I had once loved her, I thought, sinking into a depression whose cause I was unsure of.

Oddly enough, our accounts of our memories of the dead begin with the arrival of news of a sudden death. When this call comes, we are dazed, left speechless. Those who were close to the dead person may have the impression of things occurring in a dream whose meaning is out of reach. Like words heard in a dream—or rather, in a dream one was trying to recall while only half-awake. What was said, in what words? We have no idea. There are only traces of the raw reality of having been informed of something truly frightening. One's very irritation at being unable to recall the significance of words spoken in a dream feels like something that is happening in yet another dream, a nightmare. Thus, confronted with news of a sudden death, they (I) feel vertigo. Then they start to talk about you, who have already turned into a memory—about their memories of you, which are somehow lacking in reality. They emphasize the fact that you are no longer in this world as they speak of you, so the memories all become beautiful, taking on a tragic tone. Even the most boring memories are enveloped, in this place, in deep, tragic shadows.

Then I looked at the photograph, adorned with black ribbons and white chrysanthemums, of her smiling gently. I vividly remember how important it had been to me to catch even one sight of her. I had only one photo of her, and it was hard for me to look directly at her face in the photo, even when I was entirely alone. She was looking straight ahead and showing a lovely smile, so if I looked directly at it, I had the feeling that she was gazing at me, and had to avert my eyes. I had visited her home several times. I realize now that the excuses I gave for those visits must have been transparently false. I spent nights thinking of clever excuses for my visits, ones that would not seem forced but that would also not reveal my love for her. Was it that, due to these thoughts, I couldn't sleep? Or was it that I couldn't sleep, and so fantasies of visiting her house would well up until they came to seem perfectly capable of realization, and well worth carrying out; and then I would begin really to apply myself to making up good excuses? The fantasies were, finally, familiar ones, inviting a boundless, uncontrollable flood of physical images, leading to arousal and an explosive climax. She seemed willing, as on a whim, to listen to my chatter, accepting my transparent excuses, stiff, artificial, and tension-filled though they were; and it was hard to tell whether I should feel happy at that, or humiliated.

After getting on the evening train that day, I thought about how I would never see her again in this life, and, hiding my face behind the newspaper that I held spread open before me, I wept. Should I have drunk myself into a stupor as I walked about those streets, thinking of her who was dead? I had seen a movie with her once in which a man did just that. I abruptly realized that I was passionately in love with her. The train screeched over an iron bridge; the last faint paleness of twilight was swallowed up in night; and a round, pink-tinged moon began to rise.

When I remembered that, or rather, when I saw the moon, I suddenly realized that I was walking along the street with her just then, and felt utterly bewildered.

Almost all the shops in the shopping center had turned off their lights, and curtains covered the sliding glass doors at the shop entrances as well as the bright show windows that were filled during the day with toys and women's fashions and flowers. Yet all of the shops' glass doors were standing open twenty or thirty centimeters, and the skimpy, blue-and-white striped curtains swayed regularly in the breeze, now filling with wind, now falling limp. At the entrance to each and every shop, a curtain swayed in the wind; when from time to time the wind blew stronger, the wind-filled cloth curtain would blow out from between the heavy glass doors in the direction of the street and make a light, pleasant, fluttering sound, then lose its power as if suddenly exhausted and be sucked back between the glass doors. The streets of the shopping center shone with a smooth blackness, as if wet, and the wind, with mingled odors of the waters of the castle-moat just across the street, covered with duckweed, and of the trees in the park, blew through the long roadway. It still wasn't very late, but there were no pedestrians on the street, and when I realized that I was the only person walking through the long street of the shopping center, it felt very strange. It was not that I found the long, silent, deserted street frightening or dangerous, the way a small child afraid of shadows might. It was not that the shopping center was dreaming of odd shadows flitting through its streets; nor was it "all too quiet," like the lawless gunfighters' towns that one sees in Westerns, at the movies. Until a few moments ago, until just before I entered this street, there were lots of people walking about and the stores were open for business. But it occurred to me that now, suddenly, when they learned that I had come, they all might be hiding in the back of the stores with the doors locked and the lights turned out; they might be snickering there behind those curtains.

Faint lights from inside the living areas at the back of the shops that lined both sides of the street seeped out each time the curtains, blown by the wind, fluttered up as if writhing in pain; the indistinct murmurs of family conversations from the living rooms saddened me a little and made me recall a certain scene. Once, on my way back from the municipal pool, I found myself walking along an unfamiliar road and decided to try to get home by turning at every corner I came to, so that I seemed to be wandering through a labyrinth. Turning a certain corner, I entered a narrow backstreet, silent and deserted; in the listless sunlight of that summer afternoon, the sensuously drowsy light (in which even the plants in the small, confined front gardens seemed to be taking a siesta) flickered in the gentle breeze. A large mirror on the wall inside one of the houses, dimly visible through the open door, cast a pool of soft, pale reflected light over the black wooden floors of the corridor. I felt vaguely ill at ease, as if I had suddenly intruded into some stranger's quiet dreams; I was anxious lest my footsteps waken that stranger from his dreams. The thick, fleshy-leaved plants in the front garden deepened my sense of a dream. The unknown person who was having this dream was none other than me: I felt as if I had been walking the streets and then had burst into my own dream. Abruptly I was assailed by the sense that a great distance separated me from the family groups who were engaged in quiet talk there beyond the light that seeped out, faintly flickering together with the movements of the curtain. A baseless anxiety that I was far separated from them and would never be able to return assailed me and made me suddenly sad. And yet I was trying to go home! Carrying the packages Mother had told me to buy (one gutted chicken and one package of mushrooms), I was half-running along the road!

After a while I slowed my pace (or rather, stopped) and gazed from between the black rows of houses in the shopping center at the smooth round moon as it rose; wispy blue clouds that were half covered as with a fine mesh floated round the moon at a dream-like speed, giving off a faint purplish glow. Then quite abruptly, like vertigo in which the simultaneous sensations of rising and falling accompany the sudden flow of blood away from the head, a thought flashed through my mind: This moon that I was now looking at was the first moon I had seen, and at the same time, this would be the last time I would see it. Then, sensing that this present instant of thinking so would likely be quite forgotten, like so many other things, I was immensely saddened. Or would it happen that I would someday recall this present moment, this moon that I was looking at, this street and this wind, and all the sensations that I was now experiencing? I was pained by the thought that I was, instant by instant, moving away from this present instant. Time flows on without stopping and places everything irrevocably in the past—that thought made each footstep I took heavier. Still, I vowed that I would not forget anything about this moment, or anything that I had seen or thought this night. Turning back to look at the way I had come, I gazed at the curtains puffed out by the wind at each shop entrance and ruminated on the dream of those listless streets on the way back from the pool that summer afternoon. I realized I had already begun to forget most of those images, so I hurriedly gazed once more at everything in the long, desolate street of the shopping center, so as to fix it in my memory. But as I did so, the round, smooth yellow moon seemed to shift, little by little, its place above the rows of houses; and the clouds, giving off a faint purple glow like a fine-meshed bird-net, drifted far off into the distance, misting over with a grayish haze.

Then I was dismayed suddenly to discover myself recalling, as something exceedingly strange, the fact that we were now walking through the shopping center on our way to see a movie. It was the pleasant night of a day set between spring and early summer, the first day I had made a date to spend several hours alone with her. Until then I had forced myself to attend without fail the stupid, childish literary gatherings she frequented, just to catch a glimpse of her, or in the hope (how wildly my heart beat at the thought!) that I might be fortunate enough to sit next to her and exchange a few words. I would enter the tea-shop, thinking that she might be having a cup of tea there; and if there was no sign of her, I would wait patiently, hoping she would come. I did everything in my power to approach her, but my best endeavors resulted only, in the end, in the taste of humiliation. In public meetings I was able to see her and to hear her voice; and at the tea shop I could sometimes exchange smiles and nods with her. Each and every one of these slight signs of recognition made me now glad, now sad. The unconscious coquettishness she showed—so typical of a young woman—was the cause of the greatest ecstasy when I felt it was directed at me; but when it was directed at other men, I was overcome by a miserable sense of being cruelly ill used.

When I got home, I found everything just the way it had been when I left, with Mother lying on a rattan chaise-longue in her usual place in the sitting-room, listlessly reading a book with a russet cover. When she saw my face, she looked a bit angry and said, "Where were you off to, young man? I was afraid you'd been kidnapped and would never come back!" I started to open my mouth to explain what I had seen, but I was in the grip of a melancholic fretfulness and couldn't say a word. Then Father spoke: "You were looking at the moon, weren't you?" I blinked and just said "Unh" in reply. Father took the packages of food, saying, "It'll take thirty minutes to cook the chicken, so go take your bath. You're big enough to wash yourself now, but I'll wash your hair for you." It was after that that Mother died, though I don't know if it was a year after, or a month, or a week, or a day.

"Sometimes you get this vague sort of look, you know," she said. This comment was made in an irritated, mocking tone, which dismayed me all the more. In the light from the shopping center's show windows, she looked like an animal made of smooth, sleek, extremely sinuous skin, and I could feel my whole body filling with blood, like a full moon, from the lust that seethed inside me; but of course there was no way to let her know.

I was on the train with my mother. Each time the train stopped at a station, the heavy grating of the wheels against the rails traveled along the molecules of metal and made the body of the train shake, as the sound of steam escaping rose like an exaggeratedly deep sigh. When we arrived at a station, I would ask my mother if we needed to get off there or if we could keep on riding the train. "We can stay on," she'd answer; and, feeling an ecstasy of satisfaction and a deep sense of security, I'd give a loud laugh. On the return trip, Mother always had a sad look on her face. I was tired and drowsy and gave my whole body over to the comfortable, regular swaying of the train as it chugged along. My fingers felt the rough velvet of the seat, deep russet in color; and I breathed in the smell of soot and smoke mingled with the intense darkness outside, smoothly shining as if slightly wet, and the cool, moist night air that flowed in from the slightly open window. Then the round yellow moon rose, as if gliding over waters.

"After all . . ." I thought. In the seat across from mine, a man was trying to place a large piece of luggage on the metal rack above; and a sudden movement made a great number of red apples fall out of a package belonging to a young girl who seemed to have been on board since the first station. The red globes tumbled over the seats and the aisle, and, flashing a radiant pink, bounced off the head and shoulders of the girl, who had no time to dodge out of the way. The apples kept raining down to a ridiculous degree, and the young girl blushed and seemed on the point of tears as she sat there, dazed. Realizing that I had quite forgotten what words I'd intended to follow my "After all . . . ," I felt a bit strange, but started to pick up the bright red apples that were rolling down the aisle, breathing in their sweet-sour fragrance as I did so. The young girl, who was all a-twitter with surprise at what had happened, offered me several of the apples as if in apology, bowing her head over and over. I felt sorry for her, and experienced a faint flash of love.

When we got home, there was Father, a husband waiting to greet his wife, back from a long trip, with happiness disguised as disinterest, and hidden jealousy. Father looked pained and pale, hoping to glean from my words some unintended hints about the existence of a secret on Mother's part. What a strange man! But it's possible that all of that may simply be a fantasy of mine. Mother never actually went on long trips, nor did she meet someone (a young man) at some destination. Mother, to the best of my recollection, was always resting in that south-facing second-floor room, into which a soft orange light came, filtered through the shoji paper windows; or reclining on the rattan chaise-longue in the downstairs living room, with a deep rose-colored blanket over her knees. The long, long, apparently never-ending dimness of the afternoon nap—in an opaque, gloomy, slightly feverish light that was the color of home-made, pressed apple-juice—always surrounded my mother.

I constantly walked through the dimness of our house on tiptoe. In the afternoon light, as sweet-and-sour as apple juice, observing my hands and feet being dyed the same color, I now felt myself to be swimming through water.

After that, I returned home. My wife was lying on the rattan chair in the living room; raising her face from the book she was reading, she smiled: "I thought you'd be spending another night there. You haven't had dinner yet, have you?" she said. "Go on an errand for me, won't you? It's nighttime, but you can go by yourself now. The market in the shopping center stays open till nine, so go buy us a chicken and a package of mushrooms, will you?" The little boy just said, "Okay" and stood up. "So, how did it go?" my wife asked me, and I answered, "Well, there wasn't anything special, but, oh yes, a young girl on the train back gave me lots of apples . . . Anyway, how are you feeling today?"

His son came back after taking more time than he should have to go on his errand. His wife laughed and said, "Where were you off to? I was afraid you'd been kidnapped!" The little boy was about to say something, but blushing and making a face, he swallowed his words. I understood everything, and spoke: "You were looking at the moon, weren't you?" He blinked and just said "Unh" in reply.

The Boundary Line

The oppressive weight of the water boundary line. At this moment I wake up, bathed in the reflection of a forgetfulness that increases as a negative limitlessness. The dark green atmosphere after a shower, with a stifling degree of humidity. As the sleepless night expands, and one senses the breathing of the green plants silently giving off vapor, I ask myself how many nights I have gone without sleep. Distant noises from the street rise like a rosy halo in a milky ice crystal, and at times the sleepless nights become the sweat of humid pleasures, absorbed by white sheets, newly washed and giving off an odor of disinfectant. Words were swallowed together with her saliva (transparent cells, meaninglessly repeated words), spreading softly over the rose-colored roof of her mouth. Sleepless hours mingle with desire that proceeds like a madness that has its own secret order.

My habit now is to go to bed early—yes, it's true: with the passage of time, I've started to go to bed early—I usually read until I sink off to sleep. I've had the habit of reading in bed for a long time now;

true, there were several periods when the habit was suspended for a while, but even so, reading has been a kind of ritual for falling asleep since I was a child.

I decide to go to sleep, so I put a bookmark into my half-read book and turn off the light. I've been lying here in the same position for some time, and the muscles of my back and neck and arms are feeling stiff, so I stretch myself on top of the sheet, then turn over again onto my left side, bury my cheek in the pillow, and, bending my legs, draw them up against my body. Of course I can't fall asleep right away. My head is full of the book I've just been reading—of wolves in the wild, of Combrai or Wakefield. Yet there are times when I'm so tired that I fall asleep after reading only two or three pages. A rapid fall into sleep. A nosedive into slumber. Then, without fail, I wake up before morning has arrived. How unpleasant it is to wake up to darkness. It takes time to remember just where I am. My mother has taken the lamp away, so I have to move through the dark toward the door to find the light switch. The sound of the clock by my pillow. I hate putting my feet down from the bed into the darkness. I'm lying in a small, shallow boat—a small black boat on which a corpse might be laid and set adrift—and if I slowly move my hand, which is gripping one side of this soft pillow, and stretch it out along the edge, I may touch cold, viscous water that is moving slightly. Yes—she may have stretched out her hand like this and swayed her pale fingers in the midst of the soft but heavy resistance of the waves in the cold black water. She tries to put her hand a little further into the water. The heavy swell of the water. Then she leans over slightly. Her long, tangled hair, spread against her back, is drawn along each time she turns her neck, however slightly, so she takes the long, damp, heavy hank of hair in one hand and tries to shift it toward her chest. Her arms and breast and torso undulate smoothly, like waves, and her pelvis floats up into view, in the shape of a small triangle, enfolded in smooth roundness. A person's body shows countless indentations and muscles that have tensed and tightened in the oddest places. And, by the way, I of course had no idea, at the time, who she was. Then the little boat tilts in the darkness of my dream, and she is swallowed by the black waters. Her drowned corpse washes up onto the shore of my sleepless dawn.

I was not, of course, the first to discover her. Fishermen found the drowned corpse. I awoke in the middle of the night and waited anxiously for morning to come. As the hours went on, the curtain began to be dyed with a dull gray, faint radiance while night stagnated in the corners of the room and a gray gelatinous light revealed the outlines of the objects in the room in ambiguous light and shadow. But it was not yet morning. It was still night, still dark. Memories, linked together, chainlike, ordered me to forget at the same time that they ordered me to remember. My sea of sleeplessness seemed to be casting up foam due to the continual collapse and outflow of the strata of memory. (I did not see the woman's body clearly then.) The foaming edge where the sea and the land intermingle, the ambiguity of the boundary line where the waves beat and the two elements intermingle and its nearby surroundings—these were always highly sensuous to me. At the boundary everything was perfectly intermingled. On that broad expanse of gray sandy beach, one could not say where the sea began. The sea was always trying to widen its own domain, and the ground was gradually being submerged at a slow, undetectable rate. The hama-mugi and rose moss and bushes that covered the pale gray sandstone hillock and this building, looking like a large deserted ship, would finally sink to the bottom of the sea, this gray-green plain. She (the drowned corpse) would be left suspended in the temple of time. Becoming rigid, with an opaque attenuation.

Her body, asleep within the gray gelatinous light, shone with a cool, dull radiance, like a paraffin candle or a drowned corpse. The flesh, asleep, whose bluish white color floated up (or sank down), gave off a faint rainbow-colored phosphorescence, like slices of raw cod. On her breasts, round and hard like slightly dusty white porcelain, blue veins could be seen, like deep-sea trenches on some map. Did I ever tell you about my drowned corpse? About that transparent body suspended between sky and sea and sand, lying down amidst the dryness. Don't ask me to explain the significance of that pretty, drowned girl, growing stiff as she lay there, as if exhausted by a dream. I saw that grains of sand, glittering like crystal, had lodged themselves between her lips and in the whorls of her shell-like ears.

I lie in the dark and close my eyes, and my body begins to revolve, with my legs as the axis. As the speed of the revolutions gradually increases, leaning to one side, I swirl downward like a whirlpool. Inside my skull, a purple meteoric swarm bursts apart, and the shooting stars brush past each other. Horizontal vertigo assaults my heavy limbs, like the sudden capsizing of a small boat riding up and down, rolling like a buoy on the waves. Probably from anxiety or, if not, from fear (a completely childish fear, to be sure), I embrace her body as she sleeps beside me, and kiss the warm skin of her neck, on which heavy tresses of hair lie tangled, holding several strands in my lips. Her body trembles in a subtle, vague, momentary response, and the gentle, regular, mammalian beat of her heart in that heavy flesh, now made warm and tender by sleep, mingles with my veins through her perspiration-covered breasts, crushed against my chest. Her nipples, soft but a little rough, like the wet nose of an animal, are pressed lightly against my chest. In an undifferentiated solution of mingled sleep and wakefulness, she tries to slide into pleasure and once again closes her eyes. Toward her dark, seething center. Then suddenly she slips back into a deep, luscious sleep indistinguishable from pleasure. Half-lying on her side, she buries her cheek in the pillow—perspiration builds up in the compressions of her flesh, as several lines crisscross one another from her shoulder to her neck. Her body faces downward, and the arm that emerges from the blanket is bent at the elbow—she seems like a happy child, or like an animal that sleeps inside its comfortable nesting hole, curling up its hairy body and burying its nose between its legs. She lies breathing there, atop the sumptuous dining table at Nature's banquet, a place of true rest and slumber. Beads of sweat appear around her lips and hairline. Ah, her luscious, mammalian, oh-so-moving, sweet, deep sleep, that true sleep—I felt like tearing away at it with my claws.

In the shadows where flickered the edges of the blazing midsummer sky, the thought that I couldn't live without her flashed through my mind and overwhelmed me, like the assault of a sudden chill. She was, however, a woman whose vivid hues were almost dazzling; she maintained her silence with a dull coldness that swelled and surged vastly, like the world itself. Her outlines had begun to lose their clarity. They started to dissolve, turning to glass in the silver-gray roll of the waves. I tried to cling to something I could know by touch, and I felt with my hands one after another those substances that were scattered there like light. I grasped her shoulders tightly and shook her until my fingertips turned a waxen color from the strain. She seemed a bird, or a fish. The scene was watery and attenuated; the sea and sky and sandy beach all seemed like a thick, semi-transparent membrane, slack and wrinkled. Then there is that drowned corpse. And the voice that loses its words, over and over again, due to a vague will to silence, formed by rays of light refracted within someone who cannot speak. I want only to set out, and not to arrive anywhere—not anywhere at all.

The reflection of the blazing sand, dazzling beneath the scorching sun of noon, that was projected onto the screen cast a dim, flickering light on the seats in the dark theater. Stealing a glance at the seat next to me, I saw that my mother had her head down, with her hands to her forehead. I glimpsed extremely pained wrinkles on her forehead, and a slight twitching—as if by the action of a small magnet—at the outer edge of her right eyebrow, which was drawn into a frown; and I started to hate the light from the screen falling on us—the all-too empty reflections of the flames. Every time the wind blew from a side window (left open, though its black satin curtains were pulled shut) her body grew more feverish. In the middle of the movie (about a tyrannosaurus—a just-hatched baby tyrannosaurus that survived on a barren mountain in a desert region, where it was being hunted by some men), I took her out to the cinema lobby, where hard wooden benches were provided. Dysentery had been discovered in the city center, so the odors of cresol and of a strangely sweet, milky antiseptic enveloped the midsummer night like humid steam, all over the city. The dysentery itself never reached the surface of things, and seemed like a fiction: a brigade like a bacterial "sign" that advanced through the unseen roots of things, the foundational water veins, the subterranean sewers—invisible darkness. The term "polluted area" has a faintly unrealistic ring to it; it seems to be sensuously spewing forth the miasma of death and its stench. What presented itself concretely to my eyes was the fact that the dysentery epidemic was having its raw, exposed flesh covered over with cresol solution, well-boiled drinking water, and various prohibitions regarding food and fun. Of course, such an opaque and thick membrane includes an invisible porosity that opens and closes, opens and closes; and many were the children who reached those privileged, quarantined depths by perforating that thick membrane. Any number of children witnessed how the spirit of the florist's little girl, who had died after only one night's suffering, rose from the rooftop into the night sky. In a summer when one seems to be steamed alive with heat and humidity, I do nothing but sleep all day.

When I realized that the world was sliding over the particular surface that is myself with a cool, strangely bright, sleek smoothness, I felt that I was a hairless monkey, and was pained by the thought. The feverishly transpiring summer ended, and all at once the sharp tip of autumn sunlight flamed up; I received permission from my father to visit my mother in the hospital for the first time. On the tramcar seat, thickly varnished a shining amber-color, was seated a sad, fatigued-looking man, and he mumbled a few words to me, blinking his gentle eyes. "Even if she doesn't recognize you—if, for example, something like that should happen—and, well, that's how it may turn out, but even so, she might remember when she sees your face. It's not that she dislikes you or has really forgotten about you. It's just that she's gone a bit funny in the head." Seated on a hard bench in the theater lobby, my mother suddenly raised her head and smiled happily. Like a little girl who self-importantly tells a secret, she laughed deep in her throat and said, "Now, who's the one who's just come out the door of the washroom? . . . It's me! M-E, Me!" Laughing uproariously, she pointed to herself, then put one arm around my shoulders and, with a purposely wild movement, bent from her waist and gazed up into my face with a side-long look. Struggling to control my terror, to the point of tears, at her strange manner, which I was seeing now for the first time, I kept murmuring, "That's just a story, right? The start of a story you found in a book, right? Or else it must be a story you made up yourself. You've told me this story before, haven't you?"

I had a dream about the drowned corpse again, and when I woke up, I told them about it. They grimaced and responded in gloomy voices as they ran their fingers through their hair with drowsy, melancholy gestures, "Everybody has them, you know . . . dreams of a woman, or a particular scene." Then all at once I remember a woman's breast. I suddenly realize that mother's milk was being produced, foaming endlessly inside those annular veins, those bulging blue venous mountain ranges that could be seen running beneath the surface of the tense, protuberant dome. The breast seems somehow tense with pain. Madly, one of the breasts pushes between my lips and fills my mouth. But it doesn't stay there long. Of course, I could try to explain that. Of course, a subtle difference from the first one is activated, as it were mechanically, the instant that I recall it. All I can do is imagine it, or see it in words. The blue venous mountain ranges—or water veins—which, hidden inside, run over the surface of the tense, round, protuberant white dome. Perhaps we should provide words that will add an image of depth to it. The deep blue expressing depth in an ocean on a map. The blood flowing through the body like an underground water vein. I can no longer recall it at all. No, it's no use. It's gone all watery. It's totally attenuated. Its monstrous concreteness has turned to foam and melted away in the light of the sun. Nothing is left. In books, in written words, which some even call a universe, will I encounter it? There's nothing new, and, living the memory of cells that are like nested boxes, having lived with terrific speed the play of the generation of species of reptiles and amphibians and fish, I am now slowly heading toward death. In the vast world with its blurred, ambiguous boundary lines.

I encountered the drowned corpse one morning when a cool mist moistened its downy hair. When she smiled at me on the road on the outskirts of town where a grass-covered slope foaming over with dame's violet and white clover divided the train tracks and the road, I had no idea who she was. Not knowing what to do, I plucked the tender leaves of the clover from the grassy slope and bit on them with my front teeth. Her voice was made of grains of sound, very soft and low—so much so that it seemed that if one chose the very instant when they slipped from her lips, if one advanced to that level of skill, one might pick them up with one's fingers. That would be a sensuous moment for the immaculate fingers that feel only joy at the hand's mastery. When one fixes one's attention on the fingertips, purple lightning flashes. There flies to her lips and eyes a smile that flutters very rapidly, like the pinions of an owl, with its slender, breast-shaped wings. She breathed forth the grains of her voice, and thus I noticed. She no longer cares who I am. Anyone would do. It doesn't matter who is giving this account of things. Then I call her by my favorite name. I will call this drowned corpse by a name that changes moment by moment, with words that change moment by moment and are alive, moving like an animal. She will be called with words as numerous as the world itself.

Kitchen Plays

[These rooms fill with] a strange silvery light, their own twilight . . .
—Mary Norton, *The Borrowers*

The section in which all the houses were surrounded by spindle-tree hedges, forming a kind of corridor with many turns, sloped gently upward, climbing toward the sandstone hill that was at the rear of the district and that seemed as crumbly as the highest quality rice-flour cake. As he walked, turning corner after corner, along the narrow path between the spindle-tree hedges with its many zigzags, he forgot that the area was on a slope rising to the sandstone hill. He turned to the left on a path which, surrounded by spindle-tree hedges, afforded no view ahead—he knew which corner it was he'd turned, but how could he explain to someone else how to distinguish between that corner and the numberless other similar corners, without having drawn a map—or even if he had drawn one. When he turned that corner, he found a narrow gravel path that led to a front garden planted with hydrangeas. This path, however, with its gravel and hydrangeas, did not form a landmark of any kind. This was because there were as many gravel paths leading to front gardens planted with hydrangeas as there were corners, and there were any number of narrow roads that, while branching off into still smaller paths, turned generally leftwards, in the direction of the sandstone hill, and there were as many paths that were swallowed up in the caves that ran through that hill, leading to nothing in particular, as there were corners. Each time he entered this particular section in order to make his way home, he couldn't help feeling a mild anxiety about getting lost. There was a triangular stone protruding about ten centimeters from the gravel-covered ground in which it lay buried, a stone on which fine gray-green, yellow, and ocher veins ran over the triangular surface like glaciers; and he had to take care when he happened on it. He often tripped over it. Sometimes he stumbled and fell, and sometimes he was just barely able to maintain his balance and avoid falling. Then one day when he was carrying a one-liter bottle of milk, he tripped over the triangular stone and fell to the ground, breaking the bottle of milk. The white liquid was slowly absorbed into the gravel until, mixed with dust, it looked like marble-colored vomit and feces. He had to go back again to the dairy on top of the sandstone hill to buy more milk. He was already very late, but at this rate it might be nighttime before he could get home.

Since the gravel road would leave scratches on the high heels and narrow tips of her fashionable shoes—the scratches that appeared on the smooth leather of the high-heels split painfully into a number of fine lines: it looked as if globules of blood were seeping out to form faint dotted lines on the surfaces—Mother would stand at the entrance to the gravel path and shout over and over, *calling me.* She repeated her call many, many times, until he, inside the house, noticed. When he did notice, he would stop whatever he was doing and rush to get the *geta* wooden sandals that were kept just inside the front door, then carry them at a run to the entrance to the path. He must have stumbled on that triangular stone and fallen down any number of times as he did so. At the entrance to the gravel path, Mother would change from high heels to *geta.* In one hand she carried her purse; with the index and middle fingers of the other she pulled at the back straps of the high heels. In her tight-fitting doeskin suit, she walked over the gravel, her *geta* making a loud crunching sound. *Probably on my way there, I'll often stumble over that triangular stone with its gray-green and ocher veins and fall to the ground.*

After he placed the old, flat, black leather-covered box in the inner pocket of his jacket and carefully fastened the pocket opening with a large, shiny, silver-colored safety pin, his mother said, "Now you won't lose it, and you won't be pickpocketed on the tram, either." She patted the breast of his jacket, checking on the results of her little piece of workmanship with quiet satisfaction; and he felt for an instant through the cloth the touch of her hand—her large, gentle, feverish hand. "And be careful not to lose this letter, either," she continued, handing him a square white envelope, which he put into the Boston bag that already held an apple, chocolate, a sandwich, and motion sickness medicine. He shoved into a trouser pocket a wallet containing ten hundred-yen bills and ten ten-yen coins—at each step he would take, the square weight of the wallet struck against his groin, and his full-length flannel trousers made his legs itch—and was off. "When you get there, be sure to hand over the letter together with the box, and tell them it's from your mother—Yes, say, 'I've been entrusted with this by my mother.' No, make that, 'I've brought this from my mother.' A child saying 'entrusted with' would sound too affected! Just say 'brought'—that'll be fine. Anyway, everything is written in the letter, so they'll give you the money, all right. Now you be sure to put the money in your inner pocket and fasten it with this safety pin again. Be sure to pass the pin through the cloth twice, like this. You'll be all right, won't you, by yourself? Sure, you will. Now don't go wandering off anywhere, but come straight back!" *Then I was off.* On the gravel path, he stumbled over the triangular stone with veins of gray-green and ocher, and fell to the ground. One corner of the square, stiff, leather-covered case struck his ribs hard enough to leave a black-and-blue bruise later. It was still early morning, and the smell of the dust that had sunk into the earth and gravel during the night mingled with the exhalations of the trees and vegetation, leaving a sweetness in the cool dawn atmosphere; expanding his slightly painful ribcage—using the muscles that were stretched around the ribs—he breathed the sweetness in, and the pain, turning into particles, was drawn with it into the depths of his lungs. He turned numberless corners where the faint orange radiance of front-gate lights that someone had forgotten to turn off had taken on a dim, milky color, encountering no one apart from cats that slipped through the narrow spaces in the spindle-tree hedges, flattening and stretching their whole bodies in twisting wavelike motions as his chocolate-colored rubber-soled shoes passed soundlessly, catlike, over the gravel. Anxiety turned into tingling particles and climbed up his body through those rubber soles. The tingling particles, their rhythm like the ebb and flow of waves, struck against the soft wall of his skin, creating a warm sensation. It was the first time he had gone a long way by train alone, and he couldn't really believe that he would be able to reach his destination without making any mistakes, without mistaking any of the various detailed instructions he'd received. Yet he found himself on the right train, seated in a window seat on the left side, facing forward, so *I was completely, innocently at ease as I took from my Boston bag the bar of chocolate.*

It was long afterward that he recalled how he took out the chocolate bar and chewed on only one-third, carefully rewrapping the remainder in its silver foil to save it for the rest of what would be a long journey; to be more exact, it is *now* that he is recalling it. *This ambiguous moment, when I'm writing like this.* By the way, apart from the chocolate bar, he had in his Boston bag an apple and a sandwich, which must have been meant as his noon meal on the long train trip. While hoping that the trip would not come to an end, he asked a short question: "Not yet?" Since there were no adults to respond, as they always did, "We'll be there soon," without raising their eyes from the pages of the books they had started reading, he assumed the train trip would continue. After they emerged from the tunnel, the scenery outside the train window became more interesting; until then he had been bored by the fields or paddies or whatever the agricultural areas they passed through offered, finding interest only in the cattle and the horses he could see pulling plows.

Then a woman wearing a gray tweed travel outfit, who had come from a car further ahead, sat down in the seat right opposite him, despite the fact that any number of other seats were vacant. Carefully spreading the pleats out on the seat so that her skirt would not wrinkle, she opened her large black purse, took out a movie magazine, opened it, and began to read. Looking at the cover with its photo of Maureen O'Hara in a green velvet (or satin) evening gown with matching long gloves, a provocative smile on her gleaming, slightly cruel red lips, he began to feel drowsy. He had been excited and unable to sleep well last night. The motion of the train made him feel sleepy; the regular rhythm of the blood flowing through his temple, pressed against the window glass, and the up-and-down, side-to-side rhythm of the train jolted his brain with an oppressive headache that seemed to envelop him in a half-milky fog. He did not feel ill. It was not really motion sickness, but the feral odor of musk coming from the woman sitting opposite him made him feel dizzy. Then he really fell asleep, and was awakened only by a sharp, stabbing pain when, jolted forward by the shock of the train's sudden stop, he bumped his chest against the seat in front. A voice made an announcement, accompanied by the annoying static of the microphone: the train had come to a stop at a signal light, it said briefly. When he examined the area of his chest that pained him, he found that the safety pin that had kept the inner pocket of his jacket closed had pierced his chest, passing through his shirt and pinning the lining of his jacket to his skin. As he pulled the pin from his chest, he noticed that the inner pocket of his jacket was empty. Unbuttoning his shirt, he saw that a red drop of blood at the center of a bruise just below his nipple had seeped out, forming a globule that shone like a small glass bead.

When he got off the train, his feet easily touched the concrete platform, so *probably I realized that I was already an adult.* If so, perhaps his mother was already dead, and there would no longer be any need to take the money home. He grew sad, wondering what in fact he'd been doing all this time. Still, he decided to try calling home from the bank of public phones facing the bleak, dreary triangular park in front of the station.

His mother answered and said, "It's a bit out of your way, but please get a liter of milk at the dairy. There was no delivery today, for some reason. I'm feeling better today, so you can go off and play after you've brought the milk. But don't go wandering off before that, dear."

He went to the dairy at the top of the sandstone hill and got the milk from a man there who was embarrassed to have forgotten about the delivery; and then he entered a section of the path where the winding path was surrounded by spindle-tree hedges, and as he walked, turning corner after corner, the narrow road between the spindle-tree hedges, whose numerous sharp turns formed a zigzag pattern, he entirely forgot that this area was a slope that went on to the sandstone hill. He turned to the left onto a path that, hemmed in by spindle-tree hedges, afforded no view. Having turned this corner, he found that the narrow gravel path led straight to a front garden where hydrangeas were growing. There was a triangular stone with gray-green and ocher veins buried in the earth but protruding some ten centimeters from the ground-surface partly covered with gravel; he had to be careful of this stone. He often stumbled over it. Sometimes he stumbled and fell to the ground, and sometimes he barely managed to keep his balance. Then he stumbles over the triangular stone while carrying a one-liter bottle of milk and breaks the bottle. The white liquid is slowly absorbed by the gravel, coming to look like marble-colored vomit and feces as it mingles with the dust. He must turn around and go back again to the dairy at the top of the sandstone hill to buy milk.

Then he remembered the black leather case that had been stolen on the train. And the chocolate he had saved for later, carefully rewrapping it in its silver foil; and the blood, clear as a glass bead, that had seeped out in the center of the bruise just under his nipple; and Maureen O'Hara, smiling provocatively in her evening gown of satin (or velvet) the same green as her eyes; and the feral-smelling musk. His remembering that he had a mother who drank a liter of milk was so sudden and unnatural that he burst out laughing. The abruptness with which one remembers that one has forgotten even the fact of having forgotten. At this rate, he'd probably forgotten that he'd forgotten many other things. *So I think.* In this weightless space of memory. At a coffee stand in front of the station facing the triangular park where small cypress trees were planted, as he ate a doughnut—grease and powdered sugar clinging to the area around his lips—and drank some coffee.

Then he boarded the train again. It was relatively uncrowded, and every time it stopped, more passengers got off, so in the end he was the only one left. He went past many areas to the left and right of the station where the night sky was dyed faintly with an opaque light—a spindle-shaped, dusty, rose-colored fog; and he gazed at the Milky Way that flowed in the sky high above as if a wanton mistlike steam were erupting from the top of the hills whose gently sloping backs formed a black presence. The orange light on the ceiling of the car blinked on and off with the motion of the train, and sometimes it stayed off for a short while. At such times the small red bulb showing the position of the emergency stop button alone shone with a ruddy brightness, strawberry red; and he felt as if he were moving while suspended in space through the darkness of night, through a space open to the wind from all directions, impeded by nothing at all. Putting his hand into his raincoat pocket, he found cigarettes and matches and two-thirds of a chocolate bar. He put the chocolate into his mouth—it was soft, beginning to melt, and bits of tobacco and pocket fluff stuck to its surface, all of which he swallowed together; then, feeling tired, he lay down, curling himself on the shabby green velvet seat, covered with stains that gave off an unpleasant, sticky smell. The nap of the rough, threadbare velvet, stiff with dirt, pressed against his cheek, and a sticky organic smell assailed his nostrils. It was the odor of countless passengers' oily sweat and armpits, which had seeped into the cloth. The stench of all the sorts of liquids secreted from the surface of mammalian skin, something like sour milk. Liquids released into empty space, a wanton Milky Way. A Milky Way suspended in the hollows of desire, facing empty space. When he woke up, he could see the legs of the woman sitting in the seat opposite him, which were clearly revealed under the short, tight, whitish skirt, and which a soft down, like silver sprouts, enveloped in a rosy glow. The flesh of her thighs, which was drawn into the interior depths of her skirt, clothed in gray shadows, wobbled with the movements of the train: he stayed perfectly still, curled up on the seat, eager to observe the further depths. The bluely transparent veins clearly visible on the surface of the woman's thighs surged slightly, like a river flowing toward its delta. And so he decided to get off the train when the woman did. At a flower shop at the intersection in the shopping area just in front of the station, she wheedled him to buy her a bouquet of pink sweet-peas, so he got her all the pink sweet-peas that were there in a tin bucket, and *Where are you going now? I asked.*

The woman extended an arm and pointed in the direction she needed to go. *I cannot keep my eyes from the purple and blue veins clearly visible on the wrist of her extended arm.* Stunned, he directly senses the sap within her blood—the connection of her veins, bluely visible, with leaf veins. Then they turn along the road in the direction she has pointed. They walk along a canal filled with oily water and lined by gray warehouses; turning a corner, they come upon a silent, deserted street where a pale, sensuously sleepy radiance—such that even the plants in the small front gardens seem to be taking a siesta in the faint sunlight—sways in the cool breeze. Feeling a vague uneasiness, as if he had suddenly wandered into someone else's quiet dream, he worries that his footsteps may awaken the unknown other from his dream. They walk toward the entrance to a building that seems to be a rectangular warehouse whose doors, at the end of the narrow alley, have been left standing open. At the end of a long corridor that continues into the building far beyond the dim entranceway, is a large inset mirror that alone gives off a dim, dull radiance.

This apartment block-like rectangular building may, judging from its size and the height of its ceiling, have been a remodeled warehouse or school. As the number of residents increased, they had increased the number of rooms, making a kind of *ad hoc*, unplanned, as-you-like-it sort of patchwork—that was the impression given by the somehow dusty, greasy disorder of the place. The corridor twisted and turned, running abruptly into another corridor, and this was repeated until suddenly it came to a standstill in front of a door; but inside that door was a staircase. Even though he was guided along the corridor by the woman—she seemed to live there—he feared he might lose his way. On what seemed to be the third floor, after they had made several turns along a narrow corridor divided up by plywood and various other types of materials, coughing from having breathed in the accumulated dust that rose up at their every step, they finally arrived at the woman's room. From there they could see the canal, with its rainbow-colored membrane of gasoline atop black, stagnant water, and its inverted reflection of sky and clouds filled with pale afternoon light and of the storehouse on whose wall a number was written in white paint. In the bare, dreary room, the woman poured water from a big aluminum kettle into seven small empty bottles whose bottoms contained vestiges of milk gone bad, and placed the pink sweet-peas inside. But there were still lots left over, so she pulled out from beneath a large steel-framed bed a chamber pot of white enamel and put more kettle water and pink sweet-peas inside. Pushing with the back of her right hand at the moist hair clinging to her sweaty forehead and temples, she sighed in mild irritation, then gave an innocent laugh, revealing one rather appealing snaggletooth. The large steel-framed bed's springs seemed to have given out and made loud creaking sounds with every movement of their bodies: It seemed as if his interactions with the woman were being urged on by the creaking rhythm of the springs. It may have been hunger that finally woke them. The woman gazed into his face and said in a cheerful voice, "We'll go watch a play in the kitchen downstairs!" "A play in the kitchen?" he asked. "Yeah, sure. I mean, isn't that why you came here? My, but aren't you the forgetful one! And you were that way even when you were a kid . . ."

And with that, he could recall it perfectly. He had known since he was a child that there were such things. That plays were performed in the kitchen in the basement of some building. "Aren't you the forgetful one, though!" the woman said again, laughing and tossing him his clothes; and when, rushed along by her, he had finished dressing, they once again turned down those numerous dim, dusty, patched-together corridors, went down the stairs, and walked till they came to the mirror at the end of the corridor that led from the entryway to the interior of the house. The mirror, which was attached to the wall, served as a door, and when they opened it, they were standing before a stairway leading down. "I must call something to your attention," the woman said quietly, in the affected tones of an usherette in some theater. "The notion that life is a stage or theater in which time is 'spacialized,' and that it is a clown who performs there—that's a kind of universal discourse, isn't it?—but we don't use it here. Still, if you ask me just what is being performed—why, I really don't know."

As it happened, there was no performance of a play. The woman had referred to a "kitchen," and he had known about "kitchen plays" since he was a boy, so naturally he believed it would be a real kitchen, but it was just a large empty room in the basement, where the sound of waves echoed as the canal's filthy water struck against the glass window (wider than it was high) that extended across one wall, close to the ceiling. The portion of the water that was in contact with the glass window was an opaque gray, but that opaque gray also quickly melded into the heavy viscosity of the black water. The image of the moon on the surface of the water flickered palely, and a faint reflection of its radiance, moving among the waves, passed through the glass and danced upon the ceiling: It seemed as though the room were submerged in the water's dim depths. Outside the window, the bottoms of boats rushed past, and their intense force created foam and spray, the backwash making waves roil and strike loudly against the window. Then with a metallic sound, small cracks appeared in the glass; with lightning speed the cracks then spread, and water poured into the basement with terrifying force. He and the woman ran up the stairs, closed the door behind them, and raced to her third-floor room—while making many a wrong turn as they ran their seemingly haphazard course. Breathless, they threw themselves down onto the bed and fell asleep.

When they woke up in the pale light of afternoon, the woman turned over with a loud creaking of springs, gazed into his face and said in a vague tone utterly lacking in confidence, "It wouldn't be impossible for us to live here together, I suppose . . ." He could see that a guilty conscience about suggesting that something quite impossible might in fact be possible was twisting her childlike face with anxiety. "No, I've got to get back. I just remembered that I promised to get that milk to my mother." "I see. Well then, we can't live together, I guess," she said, laughing and looking relieved. "But after I take her the milk, I plan to come back here."

When he went to get milk at the dairy on top of the sandstone hill, the owner came out of his office and, apologizing for the delay in the day's delivery, gave him a bottle of milk. On the way down the hill, he entered a path hemmed in by spindle-tree hedges, turning many corners on the path, which afforded no view, and then went down a gravel path that led directly to a front garden with trees and plants. There was a triangular stone with veins of gray-green and ocher that he was always stumbling over. But he sensed that this time he would be able to return home without stumbling and breaking the bottle of milk. He felt that he wouldn't fall onto the sharp fragments of the broken milk bottle. Then he thought, *How would I explain it all to Mother?* and suddenly remembered. The fact that, long ago, he had gotten on the train together with his father and younger sister, carrying his mother's ashes, and certainly had gone to a graveyard in a town by the sea.

Picnic

> From which point on the skin does the human body
> begin, and from which point the surroundings? The air
> that comes and goes with our breathing—I cannot tell
> if it is of the inner world, or the outer. Is sweat part of
> the body, or of its surroundings?
>
> —Watanabe Kei

I remembered having promised the woman that I'd be back as
soon as I'd delivered the milk to my mother's, so I decided to return to the room. Mother drank as much as a liter of milk every
morning—grimacing, her white throat bent back, quivering at the
same rate as the liquid that flowed through it. *I become aware now*
that, having spent the whole sleepless night smoking, my tongue
is rough and the milk tastes bitter. But *I become aware now* that I
needn't worry day after day whether the milk has been properly
delivered. At any rate, I decided to return to that room after having, at the railway station shop, pressed that thick glass bottle to
my lips and teeth and poured the milk down my throat, drink-

ing it all with a grimace. The tingling sensation of the cold liquid passing through my throat. I pressed the thick bottle's mouth to my teeth and lips and, grimacing, drank it down. *I notice that I am reminded of her* by the feel of the milk bottle's thick glass. The lipstick, which had started to come off, its outlines blurred by her saliva, now remained, bright red, only at the edges of her lips—that lipstick, circular traces of which remain, as if dyed, between the vertical wrinkles of her lips—when I bite her lips lightly with my teeth, from the sides of her mouth, the muscles of which, resilient although tender and delicate, like a firm-fleshed winter cherry, are not still for an instant, shining strands of saliva flow down, tracing straight lines. The strands descend to the upturned jaw; the saliva flows diagonally down the skin as it slopes from cheek to jaw, moistening even the area of the slightly bent-back throat. Then I run the tip of my tongue over her hard, well-formed teeth and gently, carefully hold her lip between my lips and tongue, as when one softly blows across the flower of a Chinese-lantern plant cupped in one's hands.

Since there would be time until the train came—he felt that was so—he sat down on a blue bench on the train platform and lit a cigarette; he realized that it had only been one day that the milk wasn't delivered. Since the deliveryman had forgotten to bring the milk many, many times, when he returned home from school, his mother would tell him to go to the small dairy on top of the sandstone hill and get the milk from the man there, who was always embarrassed at having forgotten the delivery. On the way home, he would enter one part of a crooked path surrounded by spindle-tree hedges and walk, turning corner after corner, along the narrow path between the spindle-tree hedges, with its many zigzags; but, turning left at one point on the path that, wedged between the spindle-tree hedges, did not permit a clear sight of what was ahead, he would stumble on a triangular stone, veined with gray-green and ocher, about ten centimeters high, embedded in the surface of the gravel path, which led to a front garden where hydrangeas and oleanders were in bloom. He would tumble to the ground with the one-liter milk bottle in his hands, and the white liquid would seep slowly into the gravel, as it had done many, many times before.

"This milk comes from apple-fed cows!" the girl behind the counter of the shop on the platform suddenly said to him. Surprised, he looked her in the face. "Milk cows eat Jonathan apples, and they eat peaches, too! I suppose fruit must taste better than grass . . ." "Maybe so," he replied, and the girl nodded with a look of satisfaction and dabbed at the perspiration on her face with her white starched apron. "You come here every day, don't you?" she said. "But you never get on any of the trains." She leaned forward over the counter and, as if doing calisthenics, stretched her arms way out and grasped the counter's edge; kicking one leg back over and over, as if irritated, she finally stood on tiptoe on one foot, threw out her chest, and placed her other well-shaped leg right on top of the counter: he was quite unable to tear his eyes away from her. She held the leg steady on the countertop with both hands and started to tie the laces of her white canvas shoe, which had come undone and were dangling at the sides of the shoe. The rounded kneecap of her naked leg looked like a sweet peach, and her white arms swayed elegantly, like seaweed beneath the waters; she entwined the dangling laces around her fingers and tied them in a neat little bow. The veins on the insides of her arms are a faint blue, resembling maps of some canal system. And it is a very simple matter to discover the source of these canals. Yes—canals which run throughout the body network-fashion, with the heart as their water-source. A map of canals with a fine down growing on its surface, glistening as it mingles with a little perspiration. And so he made a date to go on a picnic with the salesgirl from the milk stand on the platform.

"Let's leave early in the morning on my day off," the girl said happily as she washed a white towel, splashing tap water against the sink. "I'll make our lunch! Which would you like? Inari-zushi, or sandwiches?"

"No, better leave the food to me. All you have to do is come along."

"But that makes things hard on you . . ."

"Never mind. You don't have to show off your lunch-making skills to me—I already like you a lot!"

The girl, her hair tightly bound up in a white cotton cloth, blushed in confusion, smiled, and then turned aside a bit pertly.

Accidents are always happening on picnics. Or if not real accidents, then it often happens that the weather changes all of a sudden, and rain starts to pour down. Or, if the weather is fine, somebody almost drowns, or is stung by a bee, or stumbles on a rock and falls down and breaks the glass insides of the thermos bottle, or cuts their finger while peeling an apple with a hiking knife from the seven-item handy-pack that they brought along quite unnecessarily, or burns themselves with the portable alcohol lamp. So I'm not sure whether I actually liked picnics or not. I was always dead tired when I got home, and I might have been shivering with the chill I got from half-drowning. Anyway, having safely made it back to my own nest, I would give a long sigh of relief. Wrapped in fold upon fold of profound sleep there in my nest. Believing (pretending to believe) in the depth of my sleep, my body curled into itself in a dog-like posture. Shut inside the depths of a sleep that permits the passage of dreams. I don't see excessively watery dreams, as of beginning to drown. My sleep resembles, rather, a dream of silently ripening peaches.

It was after my father died and we had rented out the main house to strangers, moving to the cellar-like storehouse ourselves, that we completely gave up the habit of picnicking. The picnic basket, whose English-made set of small-sized plates and cutlery for six, which Father had inherited from a great-uncle and whose components were held in place by a series of pockets and leather straps with buckles, was wrapped in brown-colored wax paper, tied with a hempen string, and stuck in the back of a cupboard. A family of six (the parents and four daughters) had come to live in the main house, and the father of that family first of all tried to dig up the triangular stone half buried in the gravel path; but, realizing that no matter how hard he dug, the stone was far too big to be unearthed, he left off midway. The younger two daughters made use of the room that I (and my late elder sister) had had, including our double-decker beds, while the elder two daughters took Father's room, which we'd always called "the study." The new renters, too, went on frequent picnics, returning home exhausted. And, noticing the unused picnic basket, which had been put out in the garden for airing, they begged to be allowed to buy it. The youngest daughter, for example, raised such a ruckus, bawling that she had to have it, that the father of the family tried to convince us to sell it, saying it was a hard-to-find item essential for their family picnics while it was *just rubbish unnecessarily taking up space in our family*, and subtly hinting that an attractive sum of money would be offered if the transaction was agreed to. But, no—it may well have been around the time of my mother's illness—and what kind of illness had it been?—when she took to her bed for so long, that our custom of going on picnics had begun to be abandoned. When I would come home, everything would be the same as when I had left, with Mother reclining on the rattan chaise-longue in the same spot in the living room, wearily reading a book with a russet cover. *When she saw me, she assumed a slightly angry look and said, "Where were you off to, you naughty child?"* Then Father, with an apron around his waist, took the bags of groceries from me, and told me to hurry up and take my bath while he made dinner, making sure to wash several key areas, *not forgetting behind your ears, your rectum, and your penis.* He told me to hurry up and take my bath: "I'll be coming in for a look later on, and if you try to get away with anything, I'll know!" My father had begun to act the part of my mother, *so I felt a creepy-crawly sort of happiness.* We could no longer go on family picnics, of course, but my father's cooking had something of the rough-and-ready quality of an outdoor meal or a picnic, and that appealed to me. Or could it have been that my mother was already in the hospital, no longer at home? Or had she perhaps run off somewhere with a younger man? Had it been my father who had run off? Having placed into his large brown suitcase his underwear, and socks rolled in on themselves into little balls, navy style, and some dress shirts, and a toilet kit containing a collapsible toothbrush with a gold handle, Father had left home one morning saying he was *off on business*, and had never come back. *We wait in vain for many days, many weeks, many months, many decades.* Father, however, may have been living by himself in a rented storehouse or annex somewhere in the depths of an area where narrow paths run their zigzag courses with numerous sharp curves; a section that extends toward the sandstone hill behind the town, sloping gently upward; a neighborhood next door, not one kilometer from his family's house, surrounded by spindle-tree hedges and fences of split bamboo, forming a kind of corridor with many turnings. Each day at the same time in the evening, there is a man who walks along the road that crosses the path in front of our house, going in the opposite direction from the hill; and *I have suspected for a long time that it is my father*. But, *did such a thing really happen?* For a picnic, one would usually have gone over the sandstone hill to the little pasture on the southern slope from which the coastline is visible, jutting out into the ocean in the form of peninsulas and islands. No—would one not, rather, have gone *away* from the sea—or, better, have boarded the bus that runs along the seacoast road, ascending the mountain road and arriving at the *artificial lake?* Avoiding the shore with the little jetty where boats could be hired and shops, rest areas, and souvenir stalls were lined up, one would have spread out on the wet grass of the opposite bank, with its somehow melancholy grove of oak trees, the frayed green picnic blanket with its many brown-colored stains, and then *we open our basket with the lunches inside.* Wouldn't this have been the time that his mother had stumbled, due to the whiskey-laced tea, and suffered a sprain? She had said she preferred going to the movies to picnics, *so, since I agreed with that,* Father buys a small movie camera and projector and makes a film entitled *Picnic.*

Having made a date to go on a picnic with the girl from the milk stand, he took a tram back home. He found that the daughters of the renter-family—all except the youngest—had married and left the house, and that the elderly parents had taken in boarders on the second floor, with its children's room and study. When, after having taken in the boarders, the elderly father told him that it was necessary for them to do so in order to pay for their youngest daughter's violin lessons, he approved their action with a gentle smile. "Oh, by all means, since it's for your daughter's sake." "You're so young, and whenever you come back, you seem to be doing so well that it makes me very envious. I only wish we had a fine, active son like you in our family. Are you in business of some kind?"

No matter how hard he looked in the storehouse, he couldn't find the picnic basket. Of course, one could go on picnics without it. Then he had a meal for the first time in a long while in his *nest coated with very dry, dusty-smelling earth.* Another suggestion by the head of the renters' household was that he should eat to-gether with their boarders, having meals prepared by the wife and daughter, since it wasn't healthy to eat only the unbalanced meals that a single man was likely to have, fecklessly choosing only foods that appealed to him. They could offer him real home-cooking, both rice and main courses, and he could pay them for it ("Just the actual costs, you understand, seeing that we have a special relationship"). He explained that he knew how to cook and sew on buttons—that he was used to doing these things for himself from childhood. "Please don't concern yourself about me. I'm a very picky eater, and I really don't care much for home-cooking anyway." The father of the household was still employed in an accountancy firm when he found out that his eldest daughter had gotten pregnant, though she was still unmarried; he hurled an apple from among those piled in a glass bowl on the dining table directly at her. This was clearly visible because the glass door of the corridor next to the sitting room, facing on the garden, was open at the time. The red globe struck the girl full on the cheek; she reeled from the blow, steadied herself on the tatami, and turned her face away. But no—it may have been the mother, reclining on her rattan chair, who suddenly raised herself and threw it at the father—that red globe, that short-distance runner of an apple that sliced through the air. The fruit that had been in the bamboo basket that he'd brought back as a souvenir of his trip. Or had it been the father who hurled it at the mother? *As a gesture in a tale of love and intense jealousy.* In any event, *the apple will certainly not be flying toward me. Unless, of course, I turn into a large insect covered in a chitin shell.* In any event, *I won't throw the apple.* And *this morning I drank the milk of a cow that had eaten apples.*

Following the subtitle *I drank the milk of a cow that had eaten my apples*, the home movie *Picnic* came to an end with a close-up of a child downing a glass of milk; or rather, with a close-up of the round, lens-like bottom of a glass and a white liquid that gradually diminishes in quantity inside the glass as it is tipped upward. The first scene in the movie opens with two apples moving up and down over and over, making a circle even as they rotate in the air. The hands that toss the apples up and then catch them, which is to say, the hands and arms that give movement to the apples, are not shown (nor is the head—a continuation of the hands and arms), so the apples appear of themselves (or by means of some mechanism) to be endlessly repeating the up-and-down motion, drawing a circle in the air even as they rotate. They seem about to fall—indeed, it's only natural that an apple should fall—but they do not. They keep on forming circles in the air with an almost acrobatic continuity, and as *we start to feel a certain fishiness and consequent unease, a kind of embarrassment, for some reason,* the apples abruptly fall to the ground and roll bouncing down the slope of the pasture. They hit one corner of the rattan picnic basket, which lies open atop the blanket, but that does not stop them: slipping through the hands that try to capture them, the two red globes roll down the slope of white clover. Then those very apples are, at the bottom of the slope, eaten up by a large red Jersey cow that is ruminating some of the white clover. In the movie *I am the one who is made to drop the apples,* but in fact, of course, that is not so. It was an entertainer who put on shows in the empty lots behind the train station that juggled the apples; and that long, beautiful, one may say, arm that reached out and tried to capture the rolling apples, that arm with its chain bracelet from which hung transparent, colorless, tear-shaped beads of glass or crystal—*resembles no one else's.*

Returning to the gray building on the banks of the canal, which looks like a warehouse or a school; returning to that maze-like building whose interior space is divided into corridors and rooms by a patchwork of plywood boards as a makeshift means of coping with the increase in residents, I saw a woman offering a glimpse of her face from a third-floor window, smiling and moving her head a little as if to nod toward him; then she quickly withdrew and closed the white muslin curtains. They did not keep out the light, so the morning radiance that came in through the curtains' weave shone like a clear gelatin that has begun to brim over, or like a blazing fire—or no, it may have shone with the vacant whiteness of a screen onto which light is projected but nothing else appears. No, not that—rather, it was perhaps shining in quite another place, quite another place. It was just in this way that the white cloth had been blown by the wind, and filled by the wind, and danced up as if writhing, and the particles of light had roiled in wild waves. I opened the large wooden door that led to the dim, humid interior of the building, and went in. What with all the turns in the corridor and the innumerable doors that lined both sides, or in certain sections only one side, of the corridor, it took me quite some time to reach her room. Or between the place where she is and *myself, there seems to be this winding corridor that maintains a constant, equal distance.* Yet it is a distance that I can overcome unconsciously, at any time; and *then I realized that I was standing always before the door of her room*! It is truly disappointing, such that it seems nothing could be simpler. Standing in front of the door of her (of their) room.

Since I adhered so very closely to her (their) body (bodies), *I couldn't tell at all where my own body began and hers (theirs) started.* Through the skin of our organs that adhered so closely to each other, the fluids seeped back and forth, and, wrapped within the tender walls of the mucous membranes—or the transparent cloth of flesh—*I discover that I myself am also a tender wall made of water.* So closely adhering, so profoundly hidden within invisible folds, *I become her (them).* Covered in sweat. Agitated by the ominous screeching sound of the bed's worn-out springs (it sounds like a voice singing, as in a bird calling or someone murmuring). *I allow my body's outlines to melt completely away.*

At last the rain will start to fall. It will become glutinous drops of water, like gray gelatin, and fall on the black surface of the water of the canal, on which floats a film of gasoline as gaudy as the pattern on a butterfly's wing; never reaching the depths at the bottom of the canal, the rain mingles with the watery surface. He notices that, though this building is extremely dusty, it has the humid and fishy atmosphere of an aquarium. "I think it might be quite possible to live here with you," she says in a vague, uncertain tone of voice. "But it's a really boring place. I often take walks inside this building. I open each and every door. Usually there's nothing inside but piles of waste paper, but it seems better than just doing nothing." "So why don't you go outside?" "Oh, I do go out sometimes, but there's not much difference, really, between here and outside." "What sort of people live here?" "What sort? Well, my family, you know . . . my parents and brothers."

He declined the woman's offer to introduce him to her family, if he liked, and went outside and began to walk in the rain. "There's a room just full of umbrellas that visitors have left behind, but I don't remember where it is, so I can't lend you an umbrella," she said with a pained expression on her face.

Then he crossed the steel bridge over the canal, went into a small Chinese restaurant in the shopping district in front of the station, and ordered a beer and some shrimp dumplings. He laughed a bit to himself, recalling how, after long experience, he had become skilled at finding cheap but good restaurants in districts he didn't know. He wondered why it was that he was so eager to find the picnic basket and fill it with food, all for the sake of the girl at the milk stand. Then the girl in the short, tight red skirt who brought the dumplings piled on a hexagonal, red-rimmed plate said in reply, "I'd much rather see a romantic love story at the movies than go on a picnic!" Surprised, he stared at her face. "I hate Nature! I don't have *any* interest at all in scenery." "But that girl is really looking forward to the picnic," he responded. "She might have been lying. Yes, I think you've been made a fool of by her." "And why would she do that?" *I get very worried.* He thinks he ought to get on a tram and go to the station where she has her stall to confirm their date, but then he notices that it's too late to go to the station.

Then he recalls that he is on his way to the hospital where his father is on the point of dying. No, not that—he recalls that he is waiting for his son to come to *the place where I lie dying.* Just now, a nurse had told him that, whisperingly: "You were the only one who didn't know! The mother of your son gave birth to a child, and kept it secret from you alone!" If one assumes that *that is a fact, a fact,* then why *was it kept secret from me alone*? Still, *I absolutely can't remember who the mother is,* and even with regard to my son, *he'd never be able to remember me anyway.* It would probably be only the movie *Picnic* that he would get to see. He wouldn't mind leaving that to his son *just as Father left it to me.* Then he said, *If I have to die, I would've liked to die in my nest.*

The Voice of Spring

In the white, narrow space between her breasts, pressed down, the sweat that seeped from their two bodies mingled, and from her breasts arose a hot mist of perfume; her body, moist and slippery with sweat, lost its clear outlines for a moment, and began to melt *in my arms.* Just as if they were in water. Her hair stuck to the beads of sweat that formed around her lips and at her forehead's hairline, and sweat collected in the five compressed lines etched on her neck, slightly bent and turned to the right. She keeps her eyes closed. When he slips his fingers through her hair, as when one sticks one's fingers into the hot wet sand on some seacoast, the heat from her skin envelops his fingers, and he tries touching the outline of her small skull, pressing down hard with his fingers. His fingers travel back and forth over the surface from the back of the head to the neck, with its compressions—over the bumps and indentations on the skin of the head, so minute that one would not know they were there without touching them. His fingers became quite wet from her sweat-soaked hair and skin, and his nostrils drank in the vegetable-based perfume that enveloped her tangled hair like hot steam. It was the smell of a summer garden gone to seed. The odor of rotting vegetation in a vaporous sea from which rise heat and the breath of innumerable plants. Then, after the woman licks at the sweat that has collected in the hollows of his shoulder blades—the sharp sensation of the tip of her tongue with its warm, slightly rough surface. Sweat and saliva mingle, crawling over the surface of the skin. "My perfume's going to stick to your skin. It'll mix with the sweat and enter through your pores," she said sensually, in a hoarse, strangled voice. He *replies*: "Never mind. There's no one who's going to cavil at it." Though *I had no intention of replying that way.*

And truly, even showering could not eliminate the odor of that perfume—clinging to his fingers and between his ribs—so he felt a bit strange. No one was caviling at it, but the smell would be absorbed by his bed sheets, along with his sweat, and would no doubt hang about his room as a slightly sour odor (the smell of a thicket of rotting vegetation). The window was small, so the ventilation in his room was poor; how would he get through the long evening calms, warmed by the radiance of a sun that never seemed to set? Fragmentary dreams revolved at a leisurely speed around his skull. The dreams slowly slipped down the hot curved surface of his skull. In a windless dream with the slightly sour scent of tendril roses and grass, as his sweat-covered temples pulsated regularly, the viscous blood continued to circulate.

"Were there really such things as 'kitchen plays'?" the man asked doubtfully. "You're jealous, aren't you?" the other responded. He answered, starting to feel more than half-suspicious of his vague sense of victory: "You're the one who's jealous. Because you didn't get to see it yourself." *I made a point of speaking in a mocking tone of voice.* "I wonder . . . Did *you* see it?" The man *responds to me* in an extremely friendly tone, so his confidence is somewhat shaken. Even if he had seen it, wasn't it just a matter of seeing the thick glass facing onto the canal in the basement room break, and seeing black water come pouring into the room. He had been familiar with the term "kitchen plays" since he was a boy—or so he had believed—but the place that he had naturally thought was a kitchen turned out to be just a large, empty basement room. But why, he wonders, did *I* know words like "kitchen plays"? "*Why did you* know that?" he asks. "Everybody knows from childhood that there are such things, and everybody thinks it strange that it is called a kitchen. But they say that it *is a fact, a fact* worthy of belief that no one has ever seen it." "What a worthless idea!" he replied. "I think so too," responded the man, and then he fell silent. *We* went over a railroad crossing and, sitting on some benches in an amusement park on the coast, just where we came out of the tunnel, we had a can of beer apiece and talked. The man said, "I'm thirsty, wouldn't you like a beer?" But he didn't pay for either of the beers, on the grounds that he had no change, and he went on to order hamburgers. The man said, handing him a hamburger wrapped in paper, "Let's go see a movie. After we finish the beer and hamburgers here, I mean." "At the theater in front of the station, right? It depends on what they're showing . . ." he replied. "I wouldn't mind seeing one if it's easy to watch." "Easy to watch, eh? If that's what you like, I think they should be showing one that'll be perfect for you. But first let's finish up these beers and hamburgers! You've lived in this town for a long time now, haven't you?" asked the man. "Yeah, I was born here. But I've never seen the whole town. There's no hill that you can see the whole town from—actually, there is a hill, but the paths to it overlap like lots of curved lines that are half-erased; and even if you climb to the top, you can't see anything, for some reason. Maybe it's because the sandstone hill itself is low and has gently rising slopes and also because houses are spread out over the slopes, with spindle-tree hedges on all sides. The area where the houses are surrounded by spindle-tree hedges, making a kind of winding corridor, gradually turns into a gentle incline and climbs toward the sandstone hill that stands behind the town, as crumbly as a high-quality rice-cake. As you walk turning corner after corner on the narrow road between the spindle-tree hedges where the many sharp turns form a zigzag pattern, you forget that this area is on an incline that leads to the sandstone hill." "If you've lived here ever since *you* were born, you must be quite familiar with the town," the man said. You turn left on a path between the spindle-tree hedges, where you can't see far ahead—I know which corner it is, but I don't know how to explain how you would distinguish it from the other countless corners of the same kind, without drawing a map—or even by drawing one. "I'm sure you don't get lost. I'm sure you don't get lost on that path with the same sort of spindle-tree hedges and pink oleanders and hydrangeas." "*I do get lost*, though. It provides no landmark, that glittering gravel path, dustily reflecting the sunlight, with its oleanders and hydrangeas heavily drooping their flowering branches in the heat. Because there are as many gravel paths leading to front gardens with the same kind of oleanders (their flowers a deep rose color) and hydrangeas as there are corners to turn; and there are many narrow roads that, while branching off into such paths, lead toward the sandstone hill, generally turning in a leftward direction; and there are as many paths that are swallowed up by caverns running through the sandstone hill without leading anywhere at all as there are corners to turn. *I walked those roads carrying a bottle of milk so many times*; and not only that: *I broke that bottle of milk so many times.*"

"The smell of my perfume will cling to you," she said, in a husky, strangled voice; I answered, "There's no one who'll cavil at it," though I had not intended to reply that way. Certainly, if the perfume—it had an exotic, incantatory name—clung and adhered fast to the skin like a hidden birthmark between the ribs or, better, around the left nipple, the next person one was with would notice. If this other perfume gave off its fragrance between the skins adhering fast to each other, moist and humid with sweat. Particularly if that next person were one's wife, *I think*, remembering that I had a wife. How had he come to leave his home? (Did he finally leave?) He really didn't know. He had said he had to go on a business trip to a town somewhere in a weaving district, and had asked his wife to pack his bag. He left the house with the bag containing a seven-item toiletries case (mold had spring up like a whitish powder sprinkled on the leather interior of the case, due to a shaving brush that had not been shaken completely dry) and a change of clothing ("I'll buy underwear when I get there, so don't bother to put any in now"). "When he left, he was wearing a bright yellow silk necktie with a brown-and-oatmeal-colored homespun jacket, a blue and white fine-checked shirt, and brown saddle shoes just bought at Maruzen" was what *Mother had always said*, wasn't it? *"Not wearing the coat, but carrying it in his hands."* "And a hat?" *I ask*, but of course I already know the answer. *"A milky tea-colored borsalino, size 7-1/8 inches."* And was it not the case that *I left my house* dressed like that? It may have been *a bit of a whim*. What might my wife be doing while I was away? How would she drink her tea, or water the flowers, or reflect on things? Was it that *I wanted to know* for sure? She sits in front of the mirror (thrusting her head forward, bringing her face close to the mirror) and applies rouge as the last element in her makeup. She spreads her lips wide to both sides, moves the little finger of her right hand left and right so as to apply the rouge evenly to the skin of her lips, then smiles at her own face in the mirror and holds that artificial smile for some time. Like a beautiful woman who keeps on smiling from the surface of a photograph. Then she relaxes the smile that has been covering the surface of her face and tries frowning like a child. Of course I don't know what she is thinking about, but *once a day, I* will no doubt steal a peek into the house from outside one of the windows, peering in at a fragment of my wife and child's lives, and then walk along the twisting, zigzag path lined by houses surrounded by spindle-tree hedges. At twilight time—yes, at twilight time in winter, when one can hear the monotonous voice of the radio announcer pronouncing in a very distinct, clipped way the state of the weather and the names of missing persons, I can see a boy looking out at me questioningly from behind a curtain. *Wasn't that me?* The man draws the brim of his gray felt hat down over his eyes and passes along the road. *I* sit in the bay window—the curtain is half-drawn—and eat some leftover bitter chocolate that I find in my pants pocket. I may have hidden myself behind the bay window's curtain in order to eat the chocolate. "You won't feel like eating your supper, again! If you eat sweets before a meal, you lose your appetite. Can't you just wait a bit?"

The man left his own cigarettes in the breast pocket of his shirt and, saying, "I'll have one, thanks," lit one of the cigarettes he had just taken out. "The movie'll be starting soon," he said. "If we leave now, we'll be just in time." They walked between the various attractions of the amusement park, deserted in the afternoon, went past a dancehall tent where two people were doing an old-fashioned fox-trot, and walked along the long concrete wall of the municipal baseball stadium. There was an epidemic of some kind in the city center, so the odors of cresole and of a strangely sweet-smelling, white, milky disinfectant were everywhere. Enveloped in the hot, humid, steamy summer, as the season neared its close, *I set out on a long journey (am setting out on a long journey)*. The long afternoon at the summer solstice seems to go on forever. In a grove of pine trees in the park across the road from the municipal baseball stadium, many lines of smoke arose as they burned the withered, rotting mountain grasses: were the fires burning the dead corpse of spring? Or perhaps they were the fires that welcome back the souls of the dead later in the summer. Maybe it had been on the afternoon of the Star Festival that he had said *I'll come back after I've taken the milk to my mother.*

The theater was hard to find. At the Silver Star, as it was called, the man said, "Look, I have tickets for two," and carefully took out and showed him two long thin slips of paper about the size of two mini-packs of Peace cigarettes lined up side by side; and on this lavender, ripple-edged flockpaper was mimeographed in crude characters: "In the event of the Silver Star Theater being crowded on Sundays or holidays, these complimentary tickets will not be honored." "The Silver Star Theater has been closed for a long time now," he replied in a slightly pitying tone—perhaps with reference to the man's anachronistic ways. "I think it was a really long time ago. There was a pyramid-shaped steel turret on the roof, with a decorative star on top, and when the wind blew, the star would revolve. I saw a movie there with Robert Mitchum as a former boxer (heavyweight, of course); but when I went back the next week, the building had already been taken down. Then a six-story building was put up on the spot." "Well but, this ticket is dated this year, and the address is on this street . . ." "Where did you get this ticket?" "I got it from the girl at the Chinese restaurant. She said since I was coming to this part of town, she'd give it to me. I'd ordered shrimp dumplings and beer, but that's what she said when she gave it to me."

It occurred to him that the Silver Star Theater might be in that six-story, by now very old and dirty concrete building, dusty and seemingly deserted as it was. On the sixth floor of that building, *his father had had his office*; and, on one of several doors lining the hallway, surely there had been a small copper plate on which the name of his father's company was embossed. On the roof was a beer garden with hanging lanterns on which the brewery's name appeared in white against a red background, and a hotel occupied the first five floors. He had been waiting for his father to come down from his office, sitting on a sofa with white linen covers in a lobby where potted lady palms were displayed. There was a canal to the rear of the building, and one could see from the lobby windows small steamboats occasionally passing by, and from the windows of the kitchen in the half-basement, he saw people hurling into the canal bucketsful of potato peels, rotten apples, coffee grounds, and other nameless garbage. For the most part the garbage made a splash and then sank right into the black water of the canal; but crescent-shaped bits of watermelon that seemed to float forever on the black surface of the water would be buffeted by the waves from the wakes of the boats, sinking and rising, alternately showing their white rinds with remnants of red flesh on which teeth marks could be seen, and their green, striped skins. *I feel thirsty.* Or I feel *a thrusting desire* toward the moist red slits where the watermelons had been cut open. Suddenly, *my father was standing behind me* and saying with a vague look on his face, "I'll treat you to some ice cream." In the hotel restaurant, the woman in the tight white skirt whom he had brought along ordered peach melba topped with currant syrup and whipped cream; that cloyingly sweet peach melba *did not appeal to me.* It wasn't that I *couldn't find* any food that did appeal: *What I wanted was a half-moon-shaped piece of watermelon.* "How old are you?" the woman asked, and when I said nothing, *Father answered* in my place.

The hotel was in severe decline, or rather, it had stopped operating as such. The lace curtains in the windows that faced onto the street had grown brown from years of sunlight and dust and hung down, torn here and there where the cloth had worn thin; on the shabby red carpet were little piles of dust and scraps of paper. The elevator didn't work, and the sofa in the lobby was broken down, with protruding springs. It seemed that mice had made nests inside it, and when they came in, a mouse raced across the floor and burrowed into a hole in the sofa. The whole place stank of mouse urine. "Is there really a theater in this building?" the man asked doubtfully. Then *I, filled with certainty*, answered, "Yes, there is."

The entrance to the Silver Star Theater was at the bottom of a stairway to the right at the end of a corridor that ran alongside the lobby. On the door was a white tile with the word "Kitchen" baked into it, held loosely in place by rusty screws.

From inside the door could be heard a woman's voice whispering, "It's about to start!" so *we pushed the door open* and went in. The reflected light from a dazzling white-hot desert beneath the blazing sun of noon, which was being projected onto the screen, cast a dim, flickering glow onto the seats in the dark theater, and by that dim light they were at last able to find two empty seats in the nearly full house. Though the woman's voice that they had heard from inside the door had said "It's about to start!" the movie in fact seemed already to have begun.

He felt, inevitably, at a loss when he *tried to write* about the movie he saw there. The audience that filled the seats had been really quiet and stiffly attentive—or at any rate, well mannered, one could say. Because when the movie ended—but what was it that really ended?—and the lights came on, what they discovered was *I*, projected onto the screen from which the rays of light that had earlier been projected there had now disappeared. Nonetheless, they did not whisper to each other and point at *me*, or steal any glances in my direction. "The smell of my perfume will cling to you," she said in husky, strangled voice; and the outlines of her body began to lose clarity, turning into a glassy thing amid the undulating silver-gray waves, and starting to melt. Only the tip of her tongue licked, with a gentle sharpness, at *the salty sweat in the hollows of my shoulder blades*. "Never mind. There's no one to cavil at this," *I* replied.

When he left the theater he lost sight of that man, and since he'd handed over his ticket to the woman standing by the door, it would be easy to claim that he'd never even seen such a movie.

I return home. He will no doubt go to the dairy on top of the sandstone hill to get the milk that the deliveryman forgot, and take it to his mother. Then he may *come back* again. From the long thin white gap between her pressed-down breasts, a mist of perfume rises, sighs quietly, and continues to increase. "The smell will cling to you," she says, or rather, *I* say—in a husky, strangled voice, and *I*, or rather, he replies, "Never mind." *My*, or at any rate someone's tongue, soft and rough, licks at the sweat in the hollows of *my*, or at any rate, someone's shoulder blades, and that becomes the water of various dreams, with sweat and saliva mingling, with liquids secreted from inside the body and semen mingling. Turning into numberless persons who are no one at all.

Poet, fiction-writer, and film critic MIEKO KANAI was born in 1947. Citing influences ranging from Borges to Jean-Luc Godard, her work is at the vanguard of contemporary Japanese prose, and her poems, stories, and essays appear regularly in major newspapers, magazines, and literary journals. This is her first book to be translated into English.

PAUL McCARTHY, Professor of Comparative Culture at Surugadai University in Japan, has translated work by Jun'ichirō Tanizaki, Takeshi Umehara, Zenno Ishigami, and Atsushi Nakajima.

SELECTED DALKEY ARCHIVE PAPERBACKS

PETROS ABATZOGLOU, *What Does Mrs. Freeman Want?*
MICHAL AJVAZ, *The Other City.*
PIERRE ALBERT-BIROT, *Grabinoulor.*
YUZ ALESHKOVSKY, *Kangaroo.*
FELIPE ALFAU, *Chromos.*
   Locos.
IVAN ÂNGELO, *The Celebration.*
   The Tower of Glass.
DAVID ANTIN, *Talking.*
ANTÓNIO LOBO ANTUNES, *Knowledge of Hell.*
ALAIN ARIAS-MISSON, *Theatre of Incest.*
JOHN ASHBERY AND JAMES SCHUYLER, *A Nest of Ninnies.*
HEIMRAD BÄCKER, *transcript.*
DJUNA BARNES, *Ladies Almanack.*
   Ryder.
JOHN BARTH, *LETTERS.*
   Sabbatical.
DONALD BARTHELME, *The King.*
   Paradise.
SVETISLAV BASARA, *Chinese Letter.*
MARK BINELLI, *Sacco and Vanzetti Must Die!*
ANDREI BITOV, *Pushkin House.*
LOUIS PAUL BOON, *Chapel Road.*
   My Little War.
   Summer in Termuren.
ROGER BOYLAN, *Killoyle.*
IGNÁCIO DE LOYOLA BRANDÃO, *Anonymous Celebrity.*
   Teeth under the Sun.
   Zero.
BONNIE BREMSER, *Troia: Mexican Memoirs.*
CHRISTINE BROOKE-ROSE, *Amalgamemnon.*
BRIGID BROPHY, *In Transit.*
MEREDITH BROSNAN, *Mr. Dynamite.*
GERALD L. BRUNS, *Modern Poetry and*
   the Idea of Language.
EVGENY BUNIMOVICH AND J. KATES, EDS.,
   Contemporary Russian Poetry: An Anthology.
GABRIELLE BURTON, *Heartbreak Hotel.*
MICHEL BUTOR, *Degrees.*
   Mobile.
   Portrait of the Artist as a Young Ape.
G. CABRERA INFANTE, *Infante's Inferno.*
   Three Trapped Tigers.
JULIETA CAMPOS, *The Fear of Losing Eurydice.*
ANNE CARSON, *Eros the Bittersweet.*
CAMILO JOSÉ CELA, *Christ versus Arizona.*
   The Family of Pascual Duarte.
   The Hive.
LOUIS-FERDINAND CÉLINE, *Castle to Castle.*
   Conversations with Professor Y.
   London Bridge.
   Normance.
   North.
   Rigadoon.
HUGO CHARTERIS, *The Tide Is Right.*
JEROME CHARYN, *The Tar Baby.*
MARC CHOLODENKO, *Mordechai Schamz.*
EMILY HOLMES COLEMAN, *The Shutter of Snow.*
ROBERT COOVER, *A Night at the Movies.*
STANLEY CRAWFORD, *Log of the S.S. The Mrs Unguentine.*
   Some Instructions to My Wife.
ROBERT CREELEY, *Collected Prose.*
RENÉ CREVEL, *Putting My Foot in It.*
RALPH CUSACK, *Cadenza.*
SUSAN DAITCH, *L.C.*
   Storytown.
NICHOLAS DELBANCO, *The Count of Concord.*
NIGEL DENNIS, *Cards of Identity.*
PETER DIMOCK, *A Short Rhetoric for Leaving the Family.*
ARIEL DORFMAN, *Konfidenz.*
COLEMAN DOWELL, *The Houses of Children.*
   Island People.
   Too Much Flesh and Jabez.
ARKADII DRAGOMOSHCHENKO, *Dust.*
RIKKI DUCORNET, *The Complete Butcher's Tales.*
   The Fountains of Neptune.
   The Jade Cabinet.
   The One Marvelous Thing.
   Phosphor in Dreamland.
   The Stain.
   The Word "Desire."
WILLIAM EASTLAKE, *The Bamboo Bed.*
   Castle Keep.
   Lyric of the Circle Heart.
JEAN ECHENOZ, *Chopin's Move.*
STANLEY ELKIN, *A Bad Man.*
   Boswell: A Modern Comedy.
   Criers and Kibitzers, Kibitzers and Criers.
   The Dick Gibson Show.
   The Franchiser.
   George Mills.
   The Living End.
   The MacGuffin.
   The Magic Kingdom.
   Mrs. Ted Bliss.
   The Rabbi of Lud.
   Van Gogh's Room at Arles.
ANNIE ERNAUX, *Cleaned Out.*
LAUREN FAIRBANKS, *Muzzle Thyself.*
   Sister Carrie.
JUAN FILLOY, *Op Oloop.*
LESLIE A. FIEDLER, *Love and Death in the American Novel.*

GUSTAVE FLAUBERT, *Bouvard and Pécuchet.*
KASS FLEISHER, *Talking out of School.*
FORD MADOX FORD, *The March of Literature.*
JON FOSSE, *Melancholy.*
MAX FRISCH, *I'm Not Stiller.*
   Man in the Holocene.
CARLOS FUENTES, *Christopher Unborn.*
   Distant Relations.
   Terra Nostra.
   Where the Air Is Clear.
JANICE GALLOWAY, *Foreign Parts.*
   The Trick Is to Keep Breathing.
WILLIAM H. GASS, *Cartesian Sonata and Other Novellas.*
   Finding a Form.
   A Temple of Texts.
   The Tunnel.
   Willie Masters' Lonesome Wife.
GÉRARD GAVARRY, *Hoppla! 1 2 3.*
ÉTIENNE GILSON, *The Arts of the Beautiful.*
   Forms and Substances in the Arts.
C. S. GISCOMBE, *Giscome Road.*
   Here.
   Prairie Style.
DOUGLAS GLOVER, *Bad News of the Heart.*
   The Enamoured Knight.
WITOLD GOMBROWICZ, *A Kind of Testament.*
KAREN ELIZABETH GORDON, *The Red Shoes.*
GEORGI GOSPODINOV, *Natural Novel.*
JUAN GOYTISOLO, *Count Julian.*
   Juan the Landless.
   Makbara.
   Marks of Identity.
PATRICK GRAINVILLE, *The Cave of Heaven.*
HENRY GREEN, *Back.*
   Blindness.
   Concluding.
   Doting.
   Nothing.
JIŘÍ GRUŠA, *The Questionnaire.*
GABRIEL GUDDING, *Rhode Island Notebook.*
JOHN HAWKES, *Whistlejacket.*
ALEKSANDAR HEMON, ED., *Best European Fiction 2010.*
AIDAN HIGGINS, *A Bestiary.*
   Balcony of Europe.
   Bornholm Night-Ferry.
   Darkling Plain: Texts for the Air.
   Flotsam and Jetsam.
   Langrishe, Go Down.
   Scenes from a Receding Past.
   Windy Arbours.
ALDOUS HUXLEY, *Antic Hay.*
   Crome Yellow.
   Point Counter Point.
   Those Barren Leaves.
   Time Must Have a Stop.
MIKHAIL IOSSEL AND JEFF PARKER, EDS., *Amerika:*
   Contemporary Russians View the United States.
GERT JONKE, *Geometric Regional Novel.*
   Homage to Czerny.
   The System of Vienna.
JACQUES JOUET, *Mountain R.*
   Savage.
CHARLES JULIET, *Conversations with Samuel Beckett and*
   Bram van Velde.
MIEKO KANAI, *The Word Book.*
HUGH KENNER, *The Counterfeiters.*
   Flaubert, Joyce and Beckett: The Stoic Comedians.
   Joyce's Voices.
DANILO KIŠ, *Garden, Ashes.*
   A Tomb for Boris Davidovich.
ANITA KONKKA, *A Fool's Paradise.*
GEORGE KONRÁD, *The City Builder.*
TADEUSZ KONWICKI, *A Minor Apocalypse.*
   The Polish Complex.
MENIS KOUMANDAREAS, *Koula.*
ELAINE KRAF, *The Princess of 72nd Street.*
JIM KRUSOE, *Iceland.*
EWA KURYLUK, *Century 21.*
ERIC LAURRENT, *Do Not Touch.*
VIOLETTE LEDUC, *La Bâtarde.*
SUZANNE JILL LEVINE, *The Subversive Scribe:*
   Translating Latin American Fiction.
DEBORAH LEVY, *Billy and Girl.*
   Pillow Talk in Europe and Other Places.
JOSÉ LEZAMA LIMA, *Paradiso.*
ROSA LIKSOM, *Dark Paradise.*
OSMAN LINS, *Avalovara.*
   The Queen of the Prisons of Greece.
ALF MAC LOCHLAINN, *The Corpus in the Library.*
   Out of Focus.
RON LOEWINSOHN, *Magnetic Field(s).*
BRIAN LYNCH, *The Winner of Sorrow.*
D. KEITH MANO, *Take Five.*
MICHELINE AHARONIAN MARCOM, *The Mirror in the Well.*
BEN MARCUS, *The Age of Wire and String.*
WALLACE MARKFIELD, *Teitlebaum's Window.*
   To an Early Grave.
DAVID MARKSON, *Reader's Block.*
   Springer's Progress.
   Wittgenstein's Mistress.
CAROLE MASO, *AVA.*

FOR A FULL LIST OF PUBLICATIONS, VISIT:
www.dalkeyarchive.com

SELECTED DALKEY ARCHIVE PAPERBACKS